The Love Surrogate

THE NOVEL

Tru Lyriq

THE WRITE ONE
PUBLISHING

TheWriteOne Publishing
ISBN: 978-0-578-68004-0

ACKNOWLEDGEMENTS

Only by your grace was I able to complete this. You have kept your word and I trust, know and believe that you will not leave nor forsake me. Father I am forever grateful for your gift and pray that I serve you well. To my mother: My rock. Though I haven't always given you peace I pray that with seeing my accomplishment you can have a piece of mind knowing that you have done everything you needed to do to help me grow as the woman you see today. I love you with all of me. Daddy: I miss you and though you aren't here to read my work, I know you always had faith in it. The times we would swap Eric Jerome Dickey books and you would swear up and down that I too would become just as great well...here's the beginning of me making you proud in heaven. To my children; Zhariun, Zavian, Skye and Shylah: my motivation. I Love You. I see me in each of you which means you are destined to be great at no matter what it may be. I have and will always support each of you as you all have done for me...WE ARE MILLIONAIRES. Mark 11:24; Speak all the desires of your hearts into existence and watch God turn those thoughts and words into actions through you. Mimi, Jimmy, Ivan, Momma V: Words cannot express how thankful I am to have you all in my life. The bonds we share are beyond inseparable. You all are the God given family that I was meant to have. It's because of each of you that I learned how to embrace who I am and make the best of life. That life is too short to be pessimistic but to walk in pride and in faith. That perfection is what we make of it and the fall is shorter than what our minds wants us to believe because when its all said and done, we are all we got. Meaca and Ashlie: through thick and thin! I see strength in yall. Even past the confusion, hurt and being misunderstood. It's something we always had in common. It takes a strong woman to endure what we have and an even stronger woman to look for solutions in the dark without knowing the outcome. From the bottom of my heart I love you both and thank you. Ashlie, Thank you for being a real friend. For looking out for me no matter what I had my hand in. You are always here when I need you and just know this is for all of us! We have something to be proud of because I would be nothing without my support system.

The
Love
Surrogate

THE NOVEL

The Love Surrogate

After years of hearing the loud 'I love you's', in the midst of the night, fade into the badgering and continuous stabbings of 'I can't stand you's' and even more torturous 'I hate you's', I learned that love doesn't have a home or keep a home happy. One thing's for sure, it has a way of packing and moving to whoever whenever. I know she loved him; loved him enough to leave a piece of herself behind, me. Her last words to me were... "take care of your daddy, he's going to need you. You're all he's got." My father loved her too; too much, I guess. From then on with each come and go of different women, I picked apart this whole "love" thing. I grew to know that no matter how many women my father courted, or how good they were at doing different things to and for him, none of them had what my mother had or could be who my mother was. I tried to fill the gaps emotionally, but as his daughter, could only do so much. At times I caught my father looking at me with disgust because of my resemblance to the only love of his life. In return, I met each of his empty yet hateful stares with a silent glance of my own. And each time, the only thing he could offer was an apology as he would down his head and walk away. I loved, well love my father deeply, and hated to see him hurt so badly, but as his child I could not give him the companionship he longed for. I don't despise my mother for leaving at all because I have grown to understand and see just how much 'love' changes a person. Too much can be dangerous but not receiving enough can kill you. My mother chose life and resisted loves pain. I watched my father die from the love sickness he carried or what we define as a broken heart. I am determined to be nothing like my mother or my father. I choose to accept loves existence, whether the concept is true or false, but I refuse to let it be the core of my life. My thoughts can only be asthmatic to the emotion but not immune. Once I get my lungs full enough to keep me going, I leave loves residue in the air for those who can bare its timeless results. Every so often I think back to the lyrics of one of my favorite songs, *'a woman's life is love and man's love is life'* but this woman has a new look on life and love. And just as love is not written in stone my heart has reconstructed itself to become one

"__Mr. Insecure__"

*Now boarding Groups 2 & 3 for flight 1535
to Dallas, Texas*
I dreaded the thought of leaving Miami. Though my heart had grown fond of the beautiful sand and chilled blue water, my time was up, and mission was accomplished.

****

Ignoring the opinions of my closest friends, Sandra and Camden, I decided what better time than the present to get my personal business off the ground. I didn't expect it to be easy to find clients in my newfound line of work, if I can call it that, but with technology and everyone dating via phone, internet or app, my services were sought in high demand. With so many avenues to choose from, I took the most obvious route in meeting new people of the opposite sex; created a singles profile on a few dating sites and just waited. My profile description on all the sites was simple: LET ME FIX YOU. I added a few details about myself with a nice profile pic and before long was in full-service mode. Now of course I didn't expect everyone to be on the same accord when I said 'Let me fix you…' because granted that could mean a number of different things. I also knew that the men I needed to deal with would be the ones to question my motive as would I. 'Mr. Insecure' was the first to do just that. After being on one of the dating sites for only 15 minutes, I had over 100 men wanting to meet me and approximately 75 of them were in my inbox. Slightly overwhelmed by the immediate response, I grabbed my notepad and wrote down the names of the potentials before reviewing their profiles individually. I could tell that a lot of them were just looking for thrills and fun, but a handful of them seemed as though they genuinely wanted what they couldn't have and lacked. This was perfect for me. I just had to find out if their 'lack' was something that I could and was willing to help with. Trying not to judge a book by its cover was my first problem. When I came across Mr. Insecure's profile, I didn't understand why a man like him would have any problems finding and keeping someone. It wasn't until he and I conversed a little via inbox that I got my answer; He suffered from the 'I blame me' complex which I found later wasn't his only problem. This part of the task would be easy, but the other issues were my concern since I was new to it all myself. As a therapist, I promised myself that I would be 100% up front with everyone I took on as a client in this new extension of my practice. It was very important that they understood that I myself am not in this for love. My intentions are solely focused on restoring faith in whatever they needed to get them through to the next relationship. Surprisingly, when I presented this proposal to him, he was 10 toes down. Told me he was willing to pay anything to erase the memories of his past to create new ones…temporary or permanent. Needless to say, we exchanged information and within a few weeks I was able to tie up the loose ends with previous clients and suspend my in-office practice to take this mini hiatus which landed me here in Miami.

Of all cities…where the most beautiful wandered the streets half naked, there was a good man who felt ugly on the inside and chose women who didn't possess what it took to make his outside beauty seep into the pores of the man himself. As a part of our agreement, he paid for my trip and was responsible for my room and board for however long necessary. When my plane landed, I was greeted by a fairly handsome driver holding roses with index cards attached to each one. Red flag number one. The woman in me rather than the therapist questioned his motives. Generally speaking, if you tend to blame yourself for the outcome of situations you know will hurt you, why would you set yourself up for that very thing to happen? The normal me was already getting annoyed by this action so I was immediately on guard. Deep down I knew there was more to what met the eye and I was being tested. Now in any other circumstance I wouldn't have taken it lightly but because I knew what I was dealing with before my arrival, I didn't entertain his childish antic and took a minute to look around for the man that craved the security he deserved. I had a small come to Jesus moment with myself.

"It's nothing personal it's strictly business."

Meanwhile, his hired driver attempted to do his job:

"You are Trinity… right?"

The way he worded his question was distasteful but rather than addressing it right away, I turned to face him and smiled gracefully, and hinted that I was no fool. He smiled in returned and gestured with his eyes in the direction of my true host. I played along for a minute developing a plan of my own.

"I am. But if you don't mind giving me a second, I think I see an old friend I want to speak to before we take off, is that cool?"

"Be my guest."

We locked eyes. Handing my bag to the driver, I walked over to him.

"Well hello."

He gazed down at the ground. Lifting his chin with my finger I repeated,

"Well hello."

With a slight grin he responded,

"Pleasure to meet you Trinity."

"So, what's this all about?"

I pointed in the direction of the driver who was exiting the airport with my luggage.

"Wanted to give you the proper introduction that's all."

"Cut the shit. You're over here playing eye spy, aren't you?"

He was speechless.

"I'm a doctor… I read through the lines for a living. I'm here to help you not hurt you and I plan on doing as much as I can when I can. I'm not here to be tested. Okay?" Without giving him time to respond, I kissed his lips. He accepted my kiss inhaling deeply. I broke our connection,

"Pleasure is all mine. Please remember, this isn't about a relationship, it's about healing. I can't help if you're going to seek a way to distrust me or the process."

"My apologies."

"None needed. Just have a little faith in me."

"Right. The Love Surrogate."

"Exactly, now let's get out of here and on to this beach."

Grabbing his hand in mine we walked out of the airport.

****

The first few days were a nightmare and completely different from what I expected and what I was used to. Minus not waking up in my usual environment, it took me a while to get used to Fabian's needy nature. Early morning texts that converted into multiple phone calls and eventually emails or the awkward pop-ups to 'make sure everything was ok'. I had to get to the root of this issue immediately because if I didn't, there was going to be a dead body in the sand, and it wasn't going to be mine. The last thing I wanted to do was question my ability to handle something I started.

"How about you come over?"

"Now? It's 5 a.m., don't you have to be up in a few hours for work?"

"I do but now that I finally have you in the same city with me…"

"Let's stop right there. This is not a real relationship. You are still supposed to do you and I am supposed to observe what the real you is like so that we can fix it…remember?"

"Yes Trinity… I am well aware that you are not my real girlfriend but how can you observe what needs to be fixed if you're not around me."

He had a point. I had been in Miami for almost a week and had only seen him twice. One being the day I landed.

"How about I meet you for lunch?"

"The car is downstairs. You don't have to get all dressed up. I'll see you in a few."

Without being given the opportunity to

respond, the line disconnected. Talking to myself,

"This is not how this works."

I rolled over and attempted to go back to sleep before my phone chimed again. Incoming text:

> **Fabian: I'm not letting you go back to sleep so get up and go downstairs...or....**

The 'or' made me think. I knew it meant that either I was going to him or he was coming to me but either way there was no way I was going to avoid seeing him. I sat up and looked around for a minute thinking to myself. How did he know that I was trying to go back to sleep? An eerie feeling crept over me as I looked in all corners of the room. Without thinking twice, I created a to-do list; refurnish apartment and check for anything or any place a camera could be hidden.

Upon arrival to his condo, I was immediately met at the door.

"So, is this what it takes to see my therapist slash acting girlfriend?"

I laughed a sarcastic laugh to myself,

"No. There is a process that..."

"Well what kind of Dr. goes..."

"Whoa!! Ok first things first. Respect. When I'm speaking please don't cut me off and secondly don't question or insult me about my profession."

Lifting his hands, he surrendered and apologized.

"Forgive me. I may have come across too strong. I was only kidding."

"Well I don't play about 2 things, my money and my food. So, what's for breakfast boo?"

"Boo? Oh, that's cute."

I figured that since I was supposed to be the 'acting girlfriend', it was time to show him a little of what she was like.

"Yeah, boo. And for the record me being the girlfriend is reserved for outings...here I am your therapist. I want to know everything; good, bad, pretty and ugly. I know we talked briefly before I got here but I also know that you haven't told me everything I need to know."

His expression changed instantly. I could tell that I had struck a nerve and the turtle was ready to retreat.

"What do you have a taste for?"

I sarcastically responded,

"Facts."

"Seriously?"

"I am serious but what else you got in the fridge?"

"Anybody ever tell you how country you sound?"

"All the time…but nice try."

Looking at Fabian I would have never guessed he was in his 40's. He was a handsome well- established man with a body that men half his age would die for. I had to suppress myself after seeing his pecs flex under his sleeveless shirt. I guess he caught me daydreaming because he broke my trance,

"Like what you see?"

"Huh?"

He laughed. I couldn't help but laugh with him.

"How you like your place?"

"It's nice. I appreciate you for putting in the time to add such intricate decorations."

"Glad you like it, but I didn't do any of that, so I can't take the credit sorry."

I figured that. It had to be a woman that decorated the place because the only way a man would have been able to create such a space is if he were…

"I'm going to ask you something and I need you to be completely honest with me."

"Ok, I'm listening?"

"Did you have my place bugged?"

I could tell my question caught him off guard but by the tone in his response, something wasn't right.

"Bugged?"

"You heard me, bugged. Did you have any form of cameras or listening devices installed around the apartment?"

He laughed to himself before shaking his head,

"You something else."

I sat quietly and waited for him to give me an answer.

"No. ok?"

I couldn't quite tell if he was lying because his mannerisms were already awkward when I first got there.

"Ok."

"Ok what?"

I shook my head and proceeded to the next subject even though I myself wasn't done.

"So, are you going to tell me the real reason why you were willing to pay for my services? I mean other than you didn't want people in your city knowing that you are desperate enough to pay for companionship from a chick you met online."

"First off, I'm not desperate, but to answer your question, my past has become so much of a constant reminder that no matter how far you come, you are still the same person they knew before. That and I've tried a little bit of everything besides this so…here we are."

"And who is they?"

He hesitated for a while before he explained what his childhood was like. I sympathized with him being the only child and not having any real friends because his mother couldn't provide the way she wanted to. He even went as far as to show me old pictures of him. I tried not to laugh but he was definitely not the man that I saw standing in front of me. Not trying to be funny but I had to ask,

"Did you have work done?"

He shook his head with disappointment.

"I'm sorry. Don't answer that. That was very unprofessional and inconsiderate of me."

"Yeah it was but no, I didn't have any work done."

He used air quotes when emphasizing the word work.

"Not even your teeth?"

"If braces count as work then that's the only thing I had done. The rest of this is all natural."

I wanted to make another joke, but something told me that it wouldn't be appropriate, so I left it alone.

"Other than the childhood that left the scar on your image, what caused the damage to your heart?"

He pushed a plate of grilled shrimp and grits in front of me with a glass of apple juice. I smiled to myself; A man that listens.

"We'll have to save that conversation for another day, I have to get ready for work…you can let yourself out. I'll have the driver take you back to your place when you're ready."

My mouth was too full to respond.

"Oh, and when you get back to your spot, I need you to decide which of the dresses you'll be wearing for tonight."

This time I managed to speak between bites,

"Tonight? What's tonight?"

"Small gala with some friends and colleagues."

"This should have been something to run by me when I first got here don't you think?"

"Why?"

"Because we have to be on one accord about my introduction."

"Introduction?"

"Yeah...how we met...how long we've known each other..."

"Oh, that's easy. We met on a dating site."

"Seriously? You plan on telling your colleagues that you met me on a dating site?"

"I already told my colleagues that I met you on a dating site."

"What the hell?"

He shook his head.

"Trinity, now days people are not ashamed of how they met the love of their lives, they're just happy that they found them."

He actually had a point. Before I could respond he looked at me and responded to my thought.

"Look they don't know that I'm paying you to be here. I don't lie very well so it's just easier for me to just leave out details that are not necessary for them to know compared to creating a whole story that I'm going to forget. I just told them that I met a beautiful therapist on an online dating site that I happened to like a lot and it just so happened you would be in town for a few months on business. I figured I would take advantage of your being here."

"Wow. The truth… twisted but true"

"Yep. It works."

"That it does."

I took a mental note on how well he twisted words. Though it was good for the moment, I knew he would try it again and it also helped me with building his character and figuring out who he was.

"Well since we're being honest, I'm going to snoop around when you leave so don't leave any embarrassing or questionable items laying around if you don't want me to know about it."

He laughed as if I were telling a joke, but I was so serious.

"That's fine but if you find any money leave it on the counter."

"Oh no! Finders keepers."

"Whatever woman."

He walked over to me and kissed me on the forehead. I had to catch myself because our chemistry was a lot stronger than I expected but made it easier for me to be me rather than be in doc mode 24-7. After he was dressed and well on his way, my stroll began.

I was careful not to pry because I saw the random cameras throughout his space but at the same time I didn't care because I gave him fair warning. Most men that kept a space like this would be considered suspect. Not that men don't like or have a taste for nice things, but his appreciation for neatness and art caught my attention immediately. His bed was neatly made, socks folded and rolled together in color or design order and everything was neatly tucked away. It was obvious that I wasn't going to come across anything laying out in the open, so I began to look through boxes and drawers. It didn't take long for me to come across old photos of him and a beautiful woman that I assumed was the ex. Just by looking at the photos you would assume they had the perfect life. With each candid shot was a new story. Holding onto a happy past could be both a blessing and a curse. Blessed to know that such times existed and cursed because you long to have them again with who may be the wrong person. Wasn't sure which emotion he was stuck in, but my observation led me to believe that this poor man was begging to be relieved of the nightmare he found himself in. Before I placed the pictures neatly back in the drawer like I had found them, I noticed a hidden latch at the bottom. There laid his true feelings. The anger and pain of torn photos and what may have been love letters and greeting cards from the one he used to adore. Not that I felt it was my place to do, but I grabbed the nearest trash can and began to empty the contents from the drawer's bottom. Step one of the healing process had already taken place.

The beginning of my journey as the Love surrogate…me and Mr. Insecure.

****

I could feel a set of eyes burning through me. I didn't recognize who she was right away until she turned and smiled at the gentleman that attempted to get her attention with small talk. I hated being put into awkward situations and started to question whether or not Fabian had brought me here purposefully as a tool to make her jealous. If so, then we had a problem. I searched the room for him, but my search was unsuccessful. I could feel my temperature rising with every glare. Luckily, I was able to suppress the little black woman in the back of my throat and was able to muster up a slight cough before returning a glance in the direction from which they came. The little woman in me screamed 'bitch can I help you' but my smile remained welcoming. Every now and then she responded to her colleague, but her eyes were locked on me. Rather than entertain the obvious, I turned around and was met instantly by Fabians chest muscles in my face. This couldn't have been a more coincidental moment for the both of us. I placed my hand in the middle of his chest and looked up into his eyes. He nodded as if my thoughts were words that escaped my mouth.

"I had no idea."

I could sense the sincerity in his voice and chose to believe that her presence was pure coincidence.

"You ok?"

"Of course. You?"

"Oh yeah. I saw you wandering off and thought I would keep an eye on you."

"Well I'm fine, despite the fact that I don't know anyone and I'm sure she's tearing me apart with her looks."

He looked over at my spectators and locked eyes with his past. His jaw clinched and eyes began to fill with sorrow. Grabbing his chin, I stole another glimpse of hurt and transferred my energy to him. Placing a soft kiss on his lips I whispered,

"Let's go handsome."

His bashful blush was timeless and so was the look on her face as we walked hand in hand away from the other party guests and towards the exit. Once we got outside and into the car, he shyly spoke.

"Thank you."

"No thank you necessary."

He smiled.

"But it is. Seeing her…"

"Breaks your heart all over again huh?"

"Yeah something like that. I just… I don't understand."

"Understand what?"

"Nothing we need to talk about now. I'm sure youll ask later."

He was right. But I had a feeling I already knew what he was getting at.

"We never do… but now that we're leaving this bourgeois party can we go get some real food and drinks?"

This time he laughed.

"Yeah. Let's do that, Ms. Greedy Lady."

I laughed.

"Sure am."

We rode in the back of the car arms linked, laughing as we shared embarrassing stories from our past relationships. I figured it would be therapeutic for him and help ease the tension of talking about what really mattered.

"When I was 13, there was this guy I had a crush on but could never talk to because my best friend always blocked anyone that showed interest in me or me in them. So, one day I decided instead of trying to approach him directly, I would make myself noticeable enough for him to want to come and talk to me. So, I got all dressed up…skirt…tank top with the cute little lace bra, makeup and all. That morning after first period, I walked past his locker and did this little shy wave thing when I passed him. And just to see if my semi-flirt action was working, I did the little slick over the shoulder look. You know just to see if he was watching me walk away and BOW…walked smack into an open locker."

He laughed hysterically. I giggled. The more he laughed the less I could. The memory soon faded to the nightmare that caused me to think of my life as less than worthy. It's crazy because my own intentions were misconstrued. What was supposed to be me telling a story to be funny turned out to be anything but and ultimately brought me back into a place that really hurt. The laughing ceased and he grabbed me.

"It's ok…we're both fine now."

He was right to a certain degree and rather than being a Debbie downer due to my own self-inflicted wound, I drowned myself in his neck. His willingness to allow me to have my way with him was dangerous because even though I'm not here to be a real girlfriend, his scent made me want to do real girlfriend things. He sensed my urge and attempted to take advantage of the opportunity that I quickly withdrew. Shortly after we pulled up to a Cuban restaurant on the corner of Collins and 7th.

"Can never go wrong with Cuban."

"This is true."

Getting out of the car and holding the door for me made me miss what a real relationship felt like. It also made it hard to believe that this man was single. I whispered to myself,

"Keep your feelings in check Trin…"

"Excuse me?"

"Oh! Nothing talking to myself. The food in here smells delicious!"

"Yeah it's my favorite go to. You should try the oxtails."

"Oxtails? Hush yo mouth, Cuban people don't eat oxtails."

We shared a laugh.

"You'll be surprised. I think they may taste better than how you all do them in Texas."

"Oh, never that. They may be good but there's nothing like a good wholesome southern smothered oxtail on white rice…"

"Well dang Ms. Hungry. I don't mean to interrupt your wet dream, but can we order before they close?"

"I'm sorry but I warned you I'm a big foodie."

"I see. Good thing it doesn't show."

"What's that supposed to mean?"

"By the way you talk about food, if I hadn't seen you, I would have thought you were over 300 pounds."

I punched him lightly on the arm.

"Ouch. See heavy handed little woman."

We laughed.

"Well since you seem to know what's good here, I'll let you order for me while I go to the little girl's room."

"Ok sweetie I got you."

The Love Surrogate

This was completely unexpected. Number one rule I had for myself…do not catch feelings. Zero. Play the part, give them what they pay for and keep it moving. This was supposed to be easy. Dabbing myself with water and looking in the mirror,

"Trinity, get it together. You are here to make this man feel secure about himself long enough to find his Mrs. Right so you can get to the next check…"

A woman exited the stall and left without even washing her hands. I gathered the last of my thoughts and exited the restroom. To my surprise, Ms. Bad Hygiene was making small talk with Fabian.

"So, you live around here?"

Her accent was thick with a Caribbean twang. I hated to come across as jealous but when I saw her reaching to touch his arm I had to interject.

"Does it matter? Hey sweet heart did you order already?"

He smiled a flattering smile before responding,

"Yes beautiful, I did."

Either Ms. "I scream for attention" didn't get the hint or she mistook herself for the Ms. Right in my rant because she kept her eyes glued to Fabian the entire time he and I spoke. Again, the little black woman in me screamed for me to give her the chance to set things straight but again I calmed her. Closing the distance between Fabian and I, she knew it was time to move around. I never knew women to be so bold and aggressive but this one was the very definition of.

"I'll see you around."

Walking past him, she slid a napkin into his hand. He followed her with his eyes then rested them back on me.

"You don't want that."

"Huh?"

I grabbed a clean napkin from the holder and covered the one she attempted to slide to Fabian with it before balling them up and throwing them away.

"Huh…she didn't even wash her hands when she left the bathroom."

"Are you serious?"

"Yep. And she just tried to pass you her number and coochie juices all at the same time."

We laughed. Him harder than me.

"You're a trip you know that?"

"Well that's what they say…so we are taking this to go right because that champagne is kicking in and I'm ready to soak it up and call it a night. We'll have to meet up in the morning to start these sessions."

"Ok, that sounds like a plan."

He took my hand into his and kissed it. We walked out of the restaurant hand in hand with smiles on each of our faces. This time I added a little extra when I saw Ms. Nasty looking in our direction. The inner me wanted to stop at her table and offer her some hand sanitizer but the grown me wouldn't let the childish me be petty and great. Once we got to the door and into the car Fabian called me out all the while laughing,

"You're so petty!"

"No! She's so nasty. That's hygiene 101. Wash your hands before leaving the bathroom. Then she's sitting at the table ready to dig her urine claws into the chips and dip."

Again, he laughed.

"Personality like no other."

"Yeah whatever. Just promise me once I get you right, you'll walk in the other direction if you see her again."

"I don't know. She was beautiful and she was feeling me."

"Are you serious right now?"

I had to stop and remember who I was dealing with.

"Never mind. You don't even have to answer that. Fabian you don't have to say yes to the first thing that gives you attention. You're worth more than you're giving yourself credit for. There are plenty of beautiful women out here and a few may be natural."

We both laughed.

"You're right she probably wasn't my type."

"Which is?"

"You."

Now he was trying to run a game that needed to be unprogrammed from his brain.

"Not to self, teach Fabian that only boys play and run games."

"So, you didn't like my line?"

I gave him a disgusted look.

"You're right she wasn't your type."

"Nope. A woman like that comes too easy. Not to mention the way women out here buy body enhancements like they're buying clothes or shoes. It's sad. Despite how desperate you think I am, I still like what I like and want what I want."

I had to give it to him because it never occurred to me that even though he was insecure in himself due to his past, he still had a straight head about what he deserved and wanted out of a woman.

"Ok...it's good to know you still have standards. Just make sure you're ready for tomorrow's session. I want 100% truth and sincerity. Deal?"

"Deal."

"Now which one of these are mine?"
He handed me a bag before I got out of the car.

"Sleep tight beauty."

"You too handsome."
Leaning over to kiss my lips, I offered my cheek instead.

"Like that?"

"Just like that."

****

And as I had suspected, he lied. Mr. Insecure had all kind of devices hidden around the place. It was going to take everything in my power not to cuss him out until I used every word in the English and Urban dictionary. I have a general understanding and some sympathy for the fact that he wasn't a cute kid so growing up and being social was difficult. But this level of insecurity for a man of his stature today is ridiculous. Hiding my true thoughts and opinions have never been my strong point and today was no exception. When the car arrived, I got in with my attitude on 500. My faithful driver was well aware and on guard.

"Everything ok this morning? You do know that I done mind telling Fabian today is not one of those days for his shenanigans."

This was the second time his informal response had caught my attention.

"You got that right! But I wouldn't just call them shenanigans...this is some bull..."

"Whoa, pretty women shouldn't talk like that."

"I'm sorry."

"No apology needed. I understand Fabian can be a bit much at times, but he means well. He's been through somethings, so he just needs to get back to the old him."

With that being said it was time to do some digging. This driver had to know a little more about Fabian than I had given him credit for and I planned on using it to my advantage.

"Oh, so you and Fabian are on a first name basis like that?"

Laughing to himself he looked at me through the rearview mirror.

"Yeah you can say that."

My curiosity started to get the best of me.

"Really? How? Better yet how long have you been driving for Fabian? And how old are you if you don't mind me asking?"

Probing I see. Well Dr. Trinity…"

I could hear the sarcasm in his voice,

"I won't tell if you won't tell."

"I'm listening…"

"I never got to introduce myself at the airport. Big bro said I was to make myself as conspicuous as possible."

"Big bro?"

He laughed again.

"Yeah. I'm something like the little brother that's bigger than the big brother."

"Biologically?"

He nodded, and I couldn't help but to laugh. The puzzle was finally coming together.

"Bamboozled! He has you driving me around like he really has a personal chauffeur."

"Oh, he does but after he had to fire his last driver for sleeping with his ex-fiancé, I offered to look out for him while you were here getting him 'fixed'."

"Wait, so you know about…"

"Yep."

I took a minute to process the part about his ex-fiancé. Information that Fabian failed to mention. I thought I was dealing with a long-time girlfriend but instead I was trying to help this man get over the woman he planned on spending the rest of his life with. Either way I found an alias who could confirm things about the man I wasn't too sure of. "So, you think I have a chance at it?"

"At what?"

"Fixing him… making him more secure about himself?"

"Look I'm not going to lie, I think the whole idea of being quote unquote fixed sounds ridiculous but, my brothers all in and I'm here for moral support not to judge. To be honest this fake thing you two got going seems too real, so you may want to check yourself to make sure you're qualified for the position of acting girlfriend."

"Excuse me?"

His blunt response was far from what I was expecting but struck a nerve too close to truth.

"Whoa relax before you chew my head off. I'm saying you may be a damn good doctor, but you're far from a player. This just doesn't seem like it's in your character. You may not think love is for you, but you clearly have voids that need to be filled too. Donating what you have you fix someone else just doesn't look right. That's just my observation from the outside looking in."

I was speechless. Had I not known any better I would've thought Camden was in the front seat and not Fabians little brother. All in all, I wasn't sure if I should be distrusting at the fact that Fabian had told his brother about me and I knew nothing of him or if I should genuinely accept the criticism from a perfect stranger about my 'performance.' It was awkward hearing someone who didn't know me from a can of paint tell me the same thing my close friends said before I started my quest into this profession/ lifestyle. It was something to think about but far from making me reconsider my new life endeavor.

"So, you know about the cameras too?"

"Cameras? This fool had cameras put in? What kind of perverted…"

"Not perverted…"

"Ooh I'm sorry…"

"Don't do that…"

"I'm saying… for somebody that's upset with what he did, you sure sound like your protecting your man."

He laughed hysterically, I didn't. Without surprise when we pulled up to Fabian's place, he had just returned from his morning jog. Looking at me and his brother suspiciously, his brother interjected.

"Hey Bro, I thought we were going running after your session."

Wide eyed he looked at his brother as if he were exposing a truth that I was still clueless about.

"Man, the gig is up ok she knows. She's a smart one. Didn't even have to threaten me to get the info. Just used her Dr. Voodoo skills and got me to talk."

I gave him a cold yet playful stare. He shrugged his shoulders and got back into the car. I walked over to Fabian with the intentions of keeping my cool but lost it.

"You lied!"

"About what?"

I held my hand out. He looked at the mini cam in the palm of my hand.

"What the hell is this?"

"Surveillance. Where'd you get that?"

"Out of the lamp in my room!"

He tried to keep his composure,

"Oh."

"Oh! That's all you have to say is oh!"

"What do you want me to say?"

"I want you to tell me why in the hell you're spying on me!"

"I'm not spying on you. I'm protecting my assets."

And before I knew it the devil on my shoulder was now dancing on my tongue. He tried calming me down several times but I let the words fly until I saw we had a small crowd gathering.

"Let's finish this inside."

"Oh, we're definitely going to do that."

Once the door to his condo closed, I was back at it.

"So, what do you have to say? I'm listening."

"I'm sorry. I just wanted to protect what I consider my investment."

Half of me understood where he was coming from and the other half of me wanted to slap the hell out of him.

"Why did you lie about it?"

"I didn't lie, I just left out a few details."

"YOU LIED! I asked you specifically if you installed cameras or listening devices at my place and you said no."

"I didn't. I purchased the items like that."
Before I knew it, I punched him the chest.

"Stop being childish! You wonder why the people in your past treat you the same despite the fact that you look different, well here's why. At this point you're still a grown ass BOY!"

"Wow."

"Yeah wow! Changing your body didn't change your mentality. No woman of worth is going to want a man this damn petty!"
I threw the camera at him. I watched his expression change from arrogant to apologetic. This man was a sympathy magnet. I knew he was playing me but the expression on his face instantly made me feel bad. My internal mini me screamed, 'Oh hell no. I'm not falling for your puppy dog eye bullshit,' but deep down I knew it was time for me to turn off my personal emotions and turn on my doctor senses. Inhaling as deeply as I could I exhaled a bitter but sincere apology.

"Let me apologize. My words may have been a little more harsh than necessary, but this is new to me just like it is to you. Yes, I am a therapist but with this hands-on practice, I'm giving a little more of me than I'm used to and it's hard to find a balance. We're going to have to help each other through this from time to time, ok?"

With his head slightly tilted down, he looked at me and nodded.

"Now, I'm not saying what you did was ok, but let this be your final warning because you're on the verge of doing this on your own if you keep doing this word twisting game and pulling these sneaky stunts. I think we've done enough playing around now it's time to get to business."

I could sense his moment of relief as I let him off the hook. I walked in first and he followed me into his office. It was a nice little set up with a cherry oak wooden desk with chairs pulled up to it. There was a beautiful chaise chair in one corner with a high back chair directly across from it in the adjacent corner. Naturally I let him take the chaise.

"Can I at least shower first?"

"Sure, but if you take too long, I'm coming in and we'll have the conversation in there."

"You promise?"

I gave him one of those 'boy if you don't get out of my face' looks.

"Ok. It'll only take a minute."

While he was across the hall in his room, I took the time to get myself together. I was so upset about finding the camera, I didn't bother with the most important parts of my wardrobe like a bra. It was a good thing that the tank I put on wasn't too thin but at some point during our conversation, I knew the cooled room would reveal my absent thoughts. I pulled out my mini recorder so that I could record our session. He came back into the room with a sweatshirt and tossed it to me. I smiled slightly; he did the same.

"Thanks."

He nodded.

"Where should I start?"

"Start wherever you like."

I didn't expect him to just jump right in but was pleasantly surprised when he did. He thought back to his childhood again; the bullying and being unable to attract the attention from the girls he crushed on all throughout school. Then he went into depth about his relationship with his parents, their divorce and how it made him want to be a better man for his family. His father wasn't exactly what you would call a rolling stone per say, but he was definitely a lady's man. He had 3 other children with other women while he was still with Fabian's mother. This horrible example caused Fabian to develop a different form neglect that contributed to his already insecure mind frame. Despite it all, his mother tried to keep what little family she thought she had together until she was just fed up completely.

"I watched my mom make dinner some nights for all of us knowing that my dad wouldn't be there, but she would do it anyway. It was hurtful to see because she knew it too. It made both of us feel like we weren't good enough even though he was the one with the issues. I kept thinking to myself like did he not want to be around because I wasn't that athletic, smooth son that men dream of having? And is that affecting his attraction to my mother who was by far the most beautiful woman he was ever with."

This was true. Looking at the pictures of his mother, she looked timeless. Much like the Nia Long's and Sanaa Lathan's out there today. Now I had a clearer understanding of the whole only child story despite the fact he does have siblings.

"So, what happened with your ex?"

He sat up on the chaise and looked around the room before focusing on me. His immediate reaction was a smile and slight giggle. That expression however shifted quickly to one that was empty yet full of pain and anger.

"If you don't want to talk..."

He put his hand up to stop me.

"She was the only thing that made sense. The only person that nurtured my introverted attitude and made me a social butterfly. The person that I liked to be rather than the person I feel I really am."

"You care to talk more about how she made you feel or what happened between the two of you?"

"No... I might as well get it out. Only a handful of people really know what happened between us."

"Your brother being one."

He shook his head no and I was instantly confused.

"Wait so your ex didn't cheat on you?"

He paused for a minute before responding.

"Only way to grow from a grown ass boy to a grown as man is to stop playing the word games right?"

I nodded with a smile. He took a deep breath and proceeded with his story.

"She and I had just gotten into an argument. She was hosting a party at her house with a couple of friends; her ex being one of the guests that she invited. She already knew how I felt about dude which pissed me off even more that she would even ask or better yet still have contact with him."

"So, this is what the argument was about?"

"Yeah that and some other things."
I took a mental note to ask about the other things after he completed his story.

"Continue…"

"When she told me that she didn't feel like it was necessary for her to get rid of people that she knew before me, it struck a nerve. I got in her face, which I knew I shouldn't have but I wasn't going to do anything because I'm not that type of guy."

"Did she know that?"

"Yeah! She would put her hands on me all the time and the only thing I could do was grab her by the wrist until she calmed down or walked away. Anyway, she got crazy on me and asked me to leave. I didn't leave right away though, she just thought I did."

"Wait how is that?"

"How is what?"

"How would she not know whether you left or not. Did you just go to your car or.." He shook his head.

"No, her house is made like this awkward 'U' shape around her pool. There's 2 actually 3 different ways you can come and go."

"Oh ok."

"I just went to the other side of the house by the pool to cool off but the whole time I was looking at her through the window."

"And she couldn't see you?"

"No, we had a little duck off spot by the pool where we used to have sex. You could see almost anywhere in the house but couldn't be seen from inside."

I nodded, and he paused as if he were thinking about something.

"I sat there a while, cooled off and when I was walking back to where she was, I saw her and her ex together. From where I was standing it looked like they were kissing but she claimed he was just looking down at her and she up at him…I wasn't convinced."

"Why is that? It sounds logical."

"Would an innocent person coming

running over screaming 'it's not what you think?'"

I could see his point, but I knew he wasn't telling the whole story.

"I see where there may have been a big misunderstanding if she wasn't allowed to explain what you thought you may have seen. Angles are deceiving."

He shook his head and sighed in disbelief, as if I had just taken her side.

"Typical."

"No. I'm just stating the obvious. Now it's very possible that you saw what you thought you saw, and it could have been that your mind was playing tricks on you as well seeing as you all had just had a misunderstanding about the same guy. Go ahead and continue with the story but before you do just know that leaving out details isn't helping you or me. He sat quiet for a while and let my words resonate in his head. I could tell that he wanted to be defensive, but I reminded him,

"Body language speaks as loud as the words you're actually saying."

He looked down at himself, then up at me as if he were confused by what I meant.

"Your whole demeanor and body language shifted while you were telling me

43

what happened. I pay attention to everything. Not just what you're saying...please continue."

He knew that I was on to his half story stunt and I could tell that he seemed slightly embarrassed about telling me the rest.

"Fabian, look, I'm not here to judge you, her, him or whoever. And I can't find the good in your goodbye if you leave out any important information so please."

This time he looked me directly in my eyes.

"When I went to the outside by the pool to cool down, I watched her through the window. I watched Nadine walk over to her..."

"Nadine?"

"Yeah. Nadine."

He downed his head and spoke softly yet angrily.

"She didn't cheat on me with her ex, not even my driver. She cheated on me with my driver's sister!"

Eyes wide I couldn't believe what I had heard. He took a deep breath and proceeded with his story.

"I hired her for dispatch. I thought it was the typical little cheer up talk you women give each other when you see the other one down. But I couldn't stop watching them.

Something didn't feel right. I just sat there and watched them until I heard some people come outside near the deck. When I got up to maneuver myself around the pool area to remain unseen, I saw what looked like shadows in her room so I logged into the cameras that I had put in her room."

"Wait, you had cameras in her place too?"

I knew my question wasn't going to make it any easier to finish his story, but I was blown away by this man and his obsession with watching people's whereabouts.

"Yes. I did."

"Did she know about them?"

"Only about the ones on the outside of the house. I didn't tell her about the ones that I had put inside."

I shook my head mentally noted his issue.

"Go ahead and continue."

He hesitated.

"Well for some reason the camera was picking up a lot of static, so I wasn't able to make out who was in the room and what they were doing so I decided to go in and see for myself. At first, I figured maybe they went into her room to escape the noise and not bring attention to the situation, but I walked in only to see her with her panties around her ankles and Nadine between her legs. I just stood there, didn't say a word. Neither of them saw me until I turned around to leave. She went out the room the other way and that's when she was approached by her ex. I stood there for a minute and watched him say something to her before he leaned down to kiss her and that's when she looked through the window and saw me heading for the front door. She rushed over claiming I didn't see what I thought I saw."

Eyes wide I gathered my thoughts and words carefully.

"So first you saw her engaged in oral sex with your driver's sister then kissing her ex?" He closed his eyes and clinched his jaw. I wanted to reach out and console him but opted not to. His insecurities were finally making sense to me. Despite the fact that he was outgrowing his physical insecurities from his childhood, they quickly took roots and grew into emotional insecurities stemming from trust.

"This may seem like a stupid question, but how did that make you feel?"

"Like a failure. Useless…my dad didn't want me as a son and now my girl was with another woman…"

I tried to stay in doctor mode, but my compassion outweighed my unbiased sympathy. I got on my knees in front of him placing my hands on his knees. I hated to say the most generic thing I could think of but he needed some form of encouragement.

"You have to understand this is not your fault and doesn't make you less than because she didn't realize what she had was good."

"Well apparently good isn't good enough and you can't tell if the grass is truly greener if you don't step out and see."

I hated that he had a way with words that really made sense. His logic was real but held no positive value to his healing.

"True. But people also have to realize that fake grass is always greener. What's real changes with the seasons, It's life. It's what makes us unique. Can you imagine what life would be like if everybody had bright green grass all the time? It's unauthentic. How would we get to see the growth in flowers? Learn the beauty in process? I have a few ideas and challenges I want you, well us to try. You down?"

"You're the Dr."

I got up from the floor and went over to my bag. Reaching in, I pulled out the index cards that I had been working on. It was an exercise that one of professors showed us that I found useful with a few of my clients back home.

"On these cards I have phrases...for instance, this one says 'I AM STRONG' on the back of this card I want you to write why. Using myself as an example...I am strong because when I had the chance to take my own life, I decided it was really time for me to live it the best way I knew how. I felt that me giving in to the feeling of being useless and lifeless made me weak so being able to do the opposite and choosing life over death is what made me strong. Does that make sense?"

He nodded.

"So, do you accept my challenge?"

He was hesitant at first but then responded, "Sure."

"Cool. There are only 7 cards here. Fill them out only when you feel you have a legitimate and positive reason to. You can take all the time you need. I will test each of these theories with your actions. Once all the cards are complete then..."

"My process is complete."

With a nod of my head I smiled. I could tell that he knew it would be a bitter sweet process but loved the fact that he knew it was one that was long overdue.

"Whenever you complete a card you can give it to me at our sessions and we can talk about it. You can complete as many cards as you like at a time. They don't have to be done individually but I want you to make sure that you really feel what you write. Cool?"

"Cool."

"Now...feed me Seymore!"

"Dang woman you always hungry!"

In my Smoky from *Friday* voice,

"And you know this mannnn..."

We both laughed. Walking toward the door,

"Trinity?"

I turned around,

"Yes..."

"When were you going to tell me that you cleaned?"

I didn't know what he meant right away until I saw him walking over to the drawer I emptied.

"You're welcome. But tomorrow is when the real cleaning begins."

He sensed what I was talking about and shook his head before following me out and to the kitchen.

****

That night, I tossed and turned. I thought about the night Camden walked in and caught me with Cyn. I never thought about being with a woman, it was against what I believed and more. But there was something about Cyn that made me feel good all the time. I wasn't sure if it was her presence or her outspoken sense of humor, but I loved being around her. On one of my home visits from college, she called me over to hang out. She was the only one from our crew that decided to stay home and go to school rather than going out of the city. It was a cool little kick back. A lot of people I knew and some I didn't. I didn't plan on drinking as much as I did, but I trusted Cyn to do right by me, which she did. She took me upstairs while the party was still jumping, got me something comfortable to sleep in and laid down with me. She understood that me drinking went two ways; either I was laughing and dancing the whole night or trapped in thoughts that destroyed me silently. She stroked my hair and wiped my tears. Told me how important I was and how she was happy to have me home. Some of the same things Camden would say but they sounded different coming from Cyn. She laid there facing me with her leg tossed over the top of mine. Her smile intoxicating. As if time were moving in slow motion, she kissed me. Soft and longingly. When her lips parted from mine, we saw Camden standing in the doorway, his eyes glistening. I attempted to sit up and go after him, but Cyn stopped me. Instead she got up and went after him. I didn't know how to feel. I wondered what was going through his mind. If he thought she and I had something or if he would understand that this was the first time I had ever been in this position. If he would look at me differently or if I would still be his Trin even though I was afraid to really be his. I sat on the balcony and looked out at the water and listened to the waves crash against the shore until I reached the bottom of the bottle.

****

"What about her? She's cute."

It was Fabian's day off and I convinced him to go to the beach with me. Despite the fact our sessions weren't moving along as I had planned, I wanted to try some other things besides the index cards. See just how insecure he was when it came to approaching random women.

"Yeah but I'm sure I'm not her type."

"And why would you say that?"

"She looks like an Instagram model. Like she's only into entertainers or athletes."

"And you look as if you could fit in either of those categories so…"

I took his book from him,

"go talk to her. At least she's natural."

"And what if she's here with someone?"

"She's not… Go!"

I pointed in her direction and reluctantly he went. Looking back occasionally to see if I was watching, I cheered him on, hinting for him to move closer to her. As expected, when he approached her, she seemed more than impressed. They talked for a while as he followed her into the water. I hated to admit but they looked good together. She was gorgeous. I could tell that she was all natural body wise but with the miracles of lace front wigs, I couldn't tell if the hair was all hers. That I was an advantage I had over her. My hair didn't rest above my behind but it was mine. I laid there and compared myself to her for so long that I didn't notice Fabian walking back.

"You good?"

I hesitated for a minute.

"Yeah. So...how did it go?"

"It went well. She's no you but she seems like the type I could get know on a deeper level."

He reached for his wallet and pulled out his card smiling. He walked back over to where she was laying and handed her his business card. She looked up at him with admiration; I felt sick to my stomach.

****

It's been roughly 3 months. Fabian and I had a few sessions after the beach and I was becoming concerned because he had only given me 2 cards. He had started talking and spending more time with what's her face, which means he was spending less time with me. As far as the card exercise, I knew that it may take some time but didn't expect it to be this long. We had professional sessions twice a week and were hanging out at least 3-4 times a week if not more; meaning we spent almost every day together. But somehow some way he made time for the other woman. I had to admit that I was enjoying every minute of it, but that didn't take away from the thought that things were becoming something more than what they were meant to be. I wanted to ask him about his progress but since I agreed that I would let him take his time with completing the challenge I never questioned it. Overall, my attraction to Fabian was growing faster than it needed to. Even though he understood we were not a real couple, he still remained attentive to my every need, as did I. I was beginning to make myself available to him at all hours of the day, thinking about him at the strangest times and even craved his attention from time to time. I knew that I was playing with fire but I'm still a woman and he is still very much a man. I removed his arm from around my waist and slid out of the bed gracefully. He shifted slightly in his sleep but never woke completely. Sliding my panties on, I exited the room and into his office. He had all the remaining cards laid out across the desk. Even though I wasn't supposed to look at them until he was ready, my curiosity got the best of me. To my surprise, all of the cards were filled out but one. Immediately I knew that my time here was being prolonged for the sake of not wanting me to leave. It was bound to happen and our actions from the previous night confirmed that.

"Simply amazing."

I jumped slightly not knowing that he was behind me.

"Didn't mean to startle you even though you're the one prying."

He took the cards from me and placed them on the far corner of the desk.

"Why haven't you given me those cards?"

"Because I'm not ready to. You said when I was 100% ready...well.."

"Well as thorough as your responses are my assumption is that you're more than ready. Don't be ashamed and hold back the progress."

"I'm not."

"So?"

He knew what I wanted to hear but refused to utter the words. Instead he walked behind me and ran his warm hands down my now chilled breasts. I placed my hands on top of his before he could go any further.

"Seriously."

He tried again to caress my bare breast with his hands and I refused his advance until he finally gave in.

"Look Trinity I know what this is. But you have taught me that when we let time heal us it will."

He quoted a part of my *open thoughts* from the contract I gave him when I started.

"And it does."

"So why haven't you let it heal you?"

I laughed to myself.

"First off, this isn't about me it's about you. But to answer your question, I don't need to be healed. I know what I want and where I want to be. Somethings aren't for everybody and love unfortunately is not for me, this is the life I choose to live. Now I understand how it's not the typical life that most people agree with or accept and I respect that."

He raised his hands as if he was surrendering and downed his head in disappointment. His psychology game was strong but still had nothing on mine.

"Don't be like that."

"Be like what? A man with a heart… compassion… sympathy?"

"Sympathy?"

"Yeah. Sympathy. I feel bad for you Trinity. You're a good woman that deserves a good man but you're too stubborn to take your own advice."
I respected his criticism but stood my ground.

"You're right I am a good woman and I have taken my own advice which is why I get pleasure out of life making good men happy and restoring what they think they lost so the next good woman can come along and get what she deserves."

"Wow."

"What?"

"You literally just took my words and flipped them to mask your twisted belief. Almost sounds like a grown ass girl instead of a grown ass woman."

"Ok…now you're going too far…let's end this conversation."

"And if I don't."

Without saying a word, I moved the chair and walked past him. Deep down I wanted him to follow me into the next room and make a fuss, but he didn't. Instead he walked over to his cards and thumbed thru them. I went into his bedroom, gathered my clothes and went into the restroom to shower. I stood in the mirror for a while until

I could barely see my reflection before walking into the standup shower and submerging my face in the water that I caught in my hands. I hated to let my mind wander and let my emotions get the best of me, but they were creeping slowly into my nerves.

"Get it together Trinity."

I whispered to myself through the water running down my face. Once I felt like myself again, I walked out of the shower, dried off and wrapped the towel around me. Instantly an eerie feeling crept over me. I opened the door to Fabians room.

"Fabian?"

No answer.

I stepped further into the dimly lit room.

"Fabian?"

I called in a sing song voice and again there was no response. I walked over to the bed with my clothes and proceeded to put them on. Right as I bent down to put my pants on, I saw the final card lying on the bed. My heart dropped into the pit of stomach. I read it aloud.

"I AM LOVED…"

Flipping the card over I proceeded.

"I am loved because you have taught me to love myself first. To look inside and be happy with the man that I have become rather than the man that everyone sees. I am loved because you love me without having to say it. Love isn't just a word, it's an action."

I turned around expecting him to be standing there like in the movies but realized I had created my own fairy tale. I finished dressing and sorrowfully left. I despised feeling the way I felt knowing that this is what I wanted. What I had planned. I helped a man gain security in himself and somehow walked away feeling less secure in myself. Once I got back to my condo, I packed my things called a cab and headed for the airport.

Now boarding Groups 2 & 3 for flight 1535 to Dallas, Texas

The attendant's voice over the intercom rang throughout the terminal. I grabbed my carry-on and walked over to the gate. Swiping my ticket across the podium I gave one final sigh before leaving my paradise. I definitely planned on coming back and leaving the business part behind.

The Love Surrogate

"<u>Mr. Needy</u>"

I wasn't quite ready to go home just yet, so I figured why not stop in a familiar yet unfamiliar place. Even though I only lived one city over, things here seemed to be so much different. But as a country girl, I loved my country twang and most importantly my country boys. When I saw how much progress Fabian was making with the challenge I gave him, I decided it was time to seek a new client. I found several prospects but opted to go with the one closest to home. I hadn't had anytime to really iron out the details with him since things ended so abruptly with Fabian, but I couldn't let that pause progression. While in the airport in Miami, I managed to find a nice and cozy little spot to rest and chill in that had open availability. Once I landed, I picked up my rental and headed to the space and as advertised it was exactly what I needed. The scenery of the downtown Dallas landscape was life and the fact that it was located near the Galleria made it even better. Nothing more perfect than to lay out at the pool and watch the sun go down and then watch the city awake when it rose again. Sitting in the window seal of the high rise, I scrolled through the pictures of my chosen client companion but was interrupted with the simultaneous buzzing of my phone. My phone had been going off non-stop since I took it off airplane mode when I landed. All messages, missed calls, and emails from Fabian and his brother.

Fabian: Where are you? Please let the me know that you're safe.
Fabian: Did I do something wrong?
Fabian: Why won't you answer my calls? I went to get us breakfast and when I came back you were gone. Why? TRINITY!!!

A few of the messages made me feel some type of way because it was as if he was calling out for me and I had abandoned him, which we both knew wasn't the case. He and I both knew that once he found the love and security in himself that he needed to press on that my job was done. Reading his messaged over and over, it was hard for me to overlook the exaggeration in his pleas. Now I admit that I should have done better with the way I chose to leave, but to be honest saying goodbye was one of those things that I was never quite good at; especially when I think about how my mom left me and my father. I made a mental note that it was probably best that I at least leave some kind of letter or note or card once I feel everything is done and my services are no longer necessary. To ease Fabians mind, I sent a very simple text.

> *Me: I'm fine. I would like to thank you for allowing me to fill the void you craved and deserved. It was truly a pleasure to work with you. I wish you the absolute best.*

Immediately after hitting send, my phone rang. I watched the phone ring until his face faded from the screen and popped up again. Deep down I wanted to answer but opted not to. Today wasn't a good day. It was best that I let things set in before he and I had an open conversation about his thoughts, feelings and the conclusion of our sessions. He was my first client so how to close things was still very new to me and how to handle my leaving was new to him. Neither of us expected my departure to be so sudden and again admitting to myself that I should have handled things a little differently was something that I needed to work on with future clients. Eventually he got the picture and my phone stopped ringing. I went into his contact settings on my phone and changed his name from 'Fabian' to 'Mr. Insecure'. I also removed his profile picture, which was something I shouldn't have done to begin with. Then I created a group titled 'Past Clients' and added his name to it. I set all call settings to my business hours and set a different ringtone for it. That way every time I finished up with a client, I could add them to the group and they would only be able to contact me during what I felt would be reasonable hours. It was time that I set some boundaries for myself and the men I chose to deal with to avoid any future mistakes like the one that had just took place. All in all, it was a lesson learned and I prayed that there would be no hard feelings between me and Fabian. The day was just about over and I needed to relax and really clear my head. I went into the bathroom, started up the jets to the Jacuzzi tub, lit whatever candles I could find and created a serene atmosphere for myself. I went over to one of my bags and found the fizzing bath bombs that Fabian had gotten me as a gift and tossed one in. Getting undressed, I walked nude across the hardwood floors and into the kitchen grabbing a wine glass and the only bottle of wine in the wine rack. I was sure it was meant to be decoration, but since I hadn't really settled in yet, it was going to have to do. Stepping into the bubbly water, steam began to emerge from my pores. Sliding down into the bubbles, I found peace. So much so that before long I had fallen asleep.

****

"Trinity! Trinity."
She frantically called my name. I ran over to where she was. Her head was sweaty and makeup smeared.
"Mommy. Are you ok?"
She downed her head.
"I want you to know that I love you dearly. Nothing in this world can change that you hear me?"
"Yes ma'am. But mommy what's wrong."
She held on to my hand. Stroking her face with it from time to time and

kissing them aggressive yet tenderly.

"Baby, mommy has to go, ok?"

"Go? Where?"

I could hear shuffling in the other room. She looked over her shoulder frightfully.

"Away. Trinity look at me baby."

I never took my eyes off hers which were now filled with tears. Deep down I knew something was wrong and no matter what I said nothing was going to change the situation at hand.

"Take care of your daddy, he's going to need you. You're all he's got."

"What about you?"

I managed to push through my own tears and trembling voice. She didn't respond. Again, we heard shuffling from the other room. She grabbed me and held me tight. I didn't want to let go. I wanted to scream 'noooo' but her body muffled my cries.

"I love you sooo much. But mommy has to go…"

I woke up gasping for air with my arms extended. My eyes full of tears. The dreams were coming back to me. Each one the same; the last conversation I had with my mother before she left me. For years I wondered why she left me behind rather than taking me with her. I wanted to hate her but couldn't. Thinking what kind of mother would leave their child with no real reason why. Not that my father was a bad man to me but apparently, he hadn't been the man my mother fell in love with. For years I cried when all my friends would attend 'Muffins with mom' for Mother's Day and I just sat in the classroom alone with the teacher until each of them returned with glowing smiles. For years I questioned what kind of woman I could or should be because the woman that was supposed to be there to show me left me to fend for myself. But with all the mixed emotions, she was still my mother. I still loved her more than life itself. I eagerly anticipated her return and willing to take her back in with open arms. That time has still never come but if it did, nothing has changed. I grew to understand it all. Sometimes life and love can be too much for people to bare especially if they feel alone or if that life/love suffocates the person they are and they lose themselves being the person everyone else expects them to be.

I was thankful for Camden. Camden was the one I thought I could love. He and I had known each other since grade school and were almost inseparable. He was there through it all, the smiles that came very seldom and the tears that eventually faded away. He shared his mother with me as I slowly developed into a woman myself. Both he and I weren't the most popular kids in school because we were so head strong and believed that if we were going to get anywhere in life we had to have the 'Degree of Relevance' in whatever field made the most money. We attended all the school functions together. So much that everyone assumed that we were either brother and sister or dating. The older we got the more difficult our relationship was to explain. I convinced him that it would be best if we both went to prom alone but rode together in the same car. He agreed. I helped him pick out his tux and he chose my dress. He and his mother took turns teaching me how to walk in heels so that I wouldn't look like a baby deer being welcomed into the world. We took the journey into adulthood together. I made him a man and he made me a woman. We were supposed to go to college together, but I couldn't stomach the thought of he and I being like my mother and father. I never wanted the fairytale ending which in my eyes was nothing but a bunch of words jumbled together on a page with an imaginary love that doesn't really exist. It wasn't until we reached the campus that I so thoughtfully told him that I wouldn't be attending Hampton University with him. Yet it was times like this that I knew I could just pick up the phone and talk to him. I already knew what he was going to say and the last thing I wanted to hear at this very moment was his criticism, but I needed him. The last time I told him about the dreams, he suggested that I talk to a professional. Well needless to say rather than speaking to one, I became one. I figured that I could help myself by helping others, which only worked for a little while. A lot of people have suffered from the same childhood neglect issues I had and seeing them cope really did help me. Camden was convinced that this new found career goal was only my way of piling more dirt on top of my own personal issues which weren't dead but very much alive. I on the other hand figured that burying the issue and looking at life in a new light was exactly what I needed. I wanted to call him and tell him about the last 3 months but immediately knew he would be disinterested seeing as he felt in his heart that I was his wife just too stubborn to accept it. Sadly, he was right about a lot of things. I'm still in ultimate denial about being any man's wife because that would suggest that I believe in love and wanted to explore whatever it has to offer. As much as I despised the subject, it also meant that I would never have children because as I have been told on many occasions having a child is a love like no other and how can I give that type of love to another life when I was deprived myself. I know that I am fully capable of filling in holes and spaces where the word love should fit, but I've also learned how to manipulate the emotion. I know I'm just not cut out for it, period. Even though I knew the turnout of the conversation I called him anyway. He answered after the first ring.

"Well hello beautiful."

There was something about the way he called me beautiful that sent chills up my spine.

"Hey bighead."

"Bighead? Oh ok."

He sensed what kind of conversation this would be.

"You ok? How you been stranger."

I stayed quiet for a while before responding.

"I'm good. You busy?"

"Yeah…busy wondering what's got my friend all in her feelings."

"Why you say that?"

I knew what he was getting at but was interested in the song that the little birds put in his ear.

"Don't play with me T. You knew I was going to find out."

"Find out what?"

"That you took a little trip out of town for business…"

"Ooh that."

I pictured him shaking his head at me in the typical Camden way.

"Yeah, that part Trinity. So what's up? This dude got you all in your feelings or what?"

"What do you mean all in my feelings?"

Again, I tried to play coy but failed miserably. He sat quietly on the phone and waited for me to continue.

"Fine! Yes, I took a mini hiatus from my clients there to take on a client out of town."

"Client?"

I was wrong. He had no idea that I had put my plan into action and already became some man's love surrogate. I sat quietly for a while waiting for him to explode, but he didn't respond.

"Yes. My client."

Again, an awkward silence.

"So…"

"So… are you going to listen or judge?"

"I'm listening Trinity."

I could hear the disappointment in his voice before I even got started. Since there really wasn't a good place to start, I just told him the whole story from beginning to the now present end. His tone was nowhere near what I thought it would be. He was calm yet concerned.

"So, you mean to tell me this man volunteered to let you play with his emotions?"

"I'm still a therapist Camden."

"Therapist huh?"

His sarcasm was really beginning to get under my skin.

"Correction. Surrogate. Isn't that what YOU called me?"

In one of the last conversations Camden and I had, he compared my brokenness and future plan to repair it to surrogacy. He called me a surrogate because like them I was willing to give something so great, then disconnect myself from it as if it were just something to do. The fact is, surrogates are able and willing to sacrifice their bodies to restore the emotions of a woman unable to bear children then they separate themselves once they have served their ultimate purpose. So, I agreed, much like a surrogate that brings life, I bring love, peace and companionship in the form of a business.

"You know I wasn't serious. If I had any idea that you would take my words and turn them into nonsense than I wouldn't have said anything at all."

"Well I guess you learned to put your foot in your mouth."

"Really Trinity, are you serious? Please hear me out because apparently you weren't listening the first time we had this conversation."

"Oh, I was listening. And I learned that I could help myself and other people at the same time."

"How can you even consider this help? Trinity, you can't be convinced that you can make a living playing with men's emotions! Do you know how much it hurts to fall in love with someone only for them to tell you they'll never really commit or that the love wasn't real?"

"There's no need for all that because they know what they're dealing with up front. I'm not going out of my way to trick anyone into filling whatever voids they need to fill. I'm just there to make the process easier. It's not about falling in love, it's about filling a void; knowing and feeling it. Hell, strippers create the same fantasy."

"Oh, so now you're comparing yourself to a stripper?"

He laughed hysterically but his laughter struck me as insulting.

"So many men turn to these dating websites to court random women they've never met. They don't know what they're going to get, love or more heartbreak. It's all a big joke. At least I come with a disclaimer and can guarantee my clients that after everything is said and done, they can have all the love and companionship they want with or without it being "real"."

"Do you hear yourself?"

"Yes, I do and for once it would be nice if you didn't judge me based on what I choose to do but support me whether you agree or disagree."

"T, baby all I'm saying is you have multiple degrees and from what I know you're doing well with just being a psychologist so why are you wanting to sink so bad?"
Biting my tongue wasn't working and before I had the chance to think twice the words came out.

"Oh, let's not talk about degrees Mr. OB/GYN turned model! You were so heartbroken after your college girlfriend left you at the dorms after graduation that you stopped practicing. Now that's love!"
I reopened a wound that had barely scabbed over. He was proud to have moved on from me and I assured him that I was happy that he was able to find someone else even though she reminded me a lot of myself. I couldn't take back what I said but I knew it cut deep.

"Wow."

"Look…I'm sorry I didn't call you to get into this spat of hurt ok. It's just that I don't need a judge right now Camden, I need a friend."
He was quiet and his whole tone changed from sarcastic to concern.

"T you know I've never been the type of person to tell you what you want to hear but what you need to hear."

"Well what I need to hear is Trinity you'll be ok. You've made it this far without her and still have so much further to go."

I pushed my words through the tears.

"Having the dreams again?"

I somberly replied,

"Yeah…"

"Well as a friend Trin, I'm proud of you and the woman you have become. I love you too much to let you fall into the wrong arms or see anything happen to you and like I told you before you need to get help baby girl because giving it isn't enough."

His words resonated in my head. In all actuality I was a hypocrite to my own belief that there is nothing wrong with seeking professional help when needed. It just sounded awkward for a psychologist to seek help in the same way I give it. I finally gave in and agreed.

"You're right."

"I'm what?"

"Camden. Seriously?"

I knew I had sung the most beautiful words in his ear, but his gloating was worse than nails on a chalk board.

"I thought I would never hear those words from you, but seriously would you like me to come with you?"

"How are you going to do that?"

"Well I'm in town for a few months and it'll be nice to see your face."

"Well I would take you up on that offer, but there's one problem."

"What's that?"

"I'm not home."

"So, you're still in Miami?"

"No, just decided that I wasn't ready to come home just yet."

"Ok, so I'm not understanding why you can't just come home. Where are you?"

I really didn't want to tell him where I was but it really didn't matter anyway.

"Dallas."

He laughed.

"Girl bring your crazy butt home. I'll see you in a few hours."

"Camden, I said I'm not ready to come home yet. I'll reach out to you when I decide to head that way. If you're still in town, I'll take you up on your offer."

"You can't be difficult all your life Trinity."

I smirked to myself.

"I think it'll probably be best if I found a doctor out here anyway. Lord knows I don't want or need half the people back home in my business."

"You're worried about the wrong thing."

"And you're never worried about anything."

"Damn right…cept one."

I knew what he was getting at.

"Boy bye."

Without giving him a chance to rebuttal and lengthen the conversation I hung up the phone. It was late and even though I was still tired, I didn't want to go back to sleep. I was afraid that if I went back to sleep, I would be faced with the same dreary vision that had made its way back into my thoughts. My mind was made up and decision was made. Whether I wanted to or not, I needed to talk to someone about my own troubles. Someone that would have an unbiased opinion of my present choices and possessed no real reason to lie to me to protect my feelings. Not that any of the people I considered to be real friends did, but I could never be too sure. Immediately the Serenity Prayer came to mind. I quoted it silently to myself before I opened my laptop and began my search for a therapist.

The Love Surrogate

"God grant me the Serenity
to accept the things I cannot
change,
Courage to change the
things I can,
And the wisdom to know the
difference."

First things first, I wanted to find a male therapist. For some reason I thought it would be a lot easier to converse with a stranger of the opposite sex than of the same sex. When we talk to someone of the opposite sex we get this imaginary sense of reassurance that they won't gossip like, hell who am I fooling, women would. We all know how women tend to be with other women and how men get around their boys. Secondly my preference is that he be black. Not that I'm racist but I figure he may be able to relate more so I wouldn't have to do a lot of explaining or answer a bunch of unnecessary questions. This I have learned from my own experience as a doctor myself. Culture plays a large part in the way we communicate, think and behave, so having someone relatable really helps. Last but far from least his work space. Now I know pickers can't be choosers or so they say but nothing is more disturbing than entering a place where you don't feel comfortable. I have gone above and beyond for a lot of my clients. For instance, my client Trish. She's an aerobics instructor so the 'office environment' freaks her out. So instead of her coming to me, I go to her. Sometimes we meet at the park with our yoga mats or in her studio and we talk over stretches or smoothies. Anything to keep her comfortable and talking, I'm down. Now it's not like I could just go to *Google* and type *black male therapist with nice office* in the search field and expect the results to lead me to my guy, so I opted to just play a game of tigers toe to narrow down my search to make my final decision.

"Dr. Joseph Isaac Ph.D. Professional Psychologist."

Saying his name out loud was surreal. Me, a psychologist, talking to another psychologist about my past so that I could be sure about my future. So that I could get to the root of these dreams and hopefully move past them rather than let them consume from time to time. The more I repeated his name aloud, the more I wasn't sure if I should be trying to talk myself out of needing the help or if I really needed it. To avoid digging myself into a bigger pit of confusion, I made the call. With each ring I became a little more nervous, there was no answer and voicemail full. I took the unusual mishap as a sign that it wasn't meant to be.

"I'm good. I can counsel myself through this like I've been doing."

Just as I was about to set my phone down and put it on the charger in the other room, it rang in my hand. For a minute I felt nauseous from the anxiety but decided to answer the call before the caller on the other end disconnected.

"Hello."

"My apologies I was just returning a call for Dr.Isaac."

Just from the sound of his voice, I knew there was a suave brother on the other end. It almost made me think twice about airing out my dirty laundry.

"Yes, I found your number online and was wondering when I could possibly come in for a session."

"Well you're actually in luck because I just had a client cancel his session for Thursday of this week so if you're available, I'm all yours."

My mind took a detour into an inappropriate place. Little did he know, his comment came out all wrong but stroked me just right. I reverted my thoughts before responding to his offer.

"Umm…sure. What time should I come in and where exactly are you located?"

He filled me in with all the details and all the while I second guessed my decision of talking about a past that was long gone. I had fought many battles and won the war, yet deep down I knew that it was important that my emotions were in check, my recent undesired dreams confirmed that.

"Ok great. I'll see you then."

Immediately after disconnecting the call, my thoughts and emotions began to clash. My thoughts were screaming all the things I wanted to hear but my feelings deflected the reality of what I was afraid to accept. Though I may have grown to accept that my past was not perfect, I am still a product of where I came from; good or bad. The certainty of my thoughts confirmed that I'm not the only person in this world that doesn't believe true love exists, but my emotions however waivered that everyone is unique in their ways. We have to be careful for what we ask for; expecting the unexpected. With a deep breath I consulted myself.

"I can do this…"

Just to complete my mental check list, I grabbed my laptop and put the address he gave me into maps to get an aerial view of his place. I realized that the address he provided was different from the address that was listed online along with his doctor profile, so to be on the safe side, I read the reviews just to make sure that I wasn't falling for some pervert advertising himself as someone he was not. The views of both locations seemed legitimate and professional, though one seemed a little more intimate than the other, but my main concern was the internal atmosphere. I prayed that Dr. Isaac was not one of those TV doctors but was still knowledgeable and passionate about his craft. Only time would tell and I only had a day to gather my thoughts before I took that giant step that I have watched so many of my clients take. Laying across the bed, I fought my sleep until the sand man won.

****

Beep. Beep. Beep.
Rolling over and forcing myself out of bed, I grabbed my satin robe off the hook and headed to the shower. The longer I stood in

the steam smothering water, the more Camden's words echoed in my head. Getting out of the shower and prepping myself, I looked at my reflection in the mirror and was instantly greeted by fear.

"What the hell am I doing?"

I stood there for a minute as if I was waiting for my reflection to respond. Shaking off the fear that had slowly covered my shoulders like a cloak, I added the final touches to my makeup and said a small prayer.

Father God I would like to thank you for waking me this morning and starting me on my way. I don't know what you have instore for me but I have faith that whatever comes from this is a lesson of growth from you. What is for me is for me and with you all things are possible… Amen

Your destination is on the right.

It was nothing like I had anticipated. I turned right into the gated property that consisted of personal condominiums. I sat outside his office for a minute to gather my thoughts and give myself one last glance in the visor.

I took short choppy steps toward the door of his business condo. Reaching for the door handle, it opened. There he stood 6 foot something with the smile to die for. Although I had pictured a brother by the tone in his voice, this gorgeous Latin man had all the attributes to drive a woman crazy, starting with me.

"Well good morning."

"Good morning to you as well."

We stood silently admiring each other. He had this hood brother swag about him that came a little too natural and spoke in volumes. His tight fitted 'V' neck t-shirt outlined his muscular frame and toned arms. The jeans he wore sat perfectly on his waist line with a natural sag. In my head I imagined Will Lemay standing in front of me and my hands touring the body that I knew was flawless. I broke the silence and extended my hand to him.

"A token of my appreciation for meeting with me on such short notice."

I offered the cup of coffee and he accepted with a slight blush.

"Thank you. I guess great minds think a like because I just made us some of my award winning cappuccino."

He opened the door wider revealing a cappuccino maker with two mugs.

"So you plan on coming in or just standing there because this Texas heat plays no games."

Snapping back into reality he wasn't lying. I could feel beads of sweat forming in the small of my back. I shook off my amazement and walked in on his command. I stood just short of the doors entry allowing him enough space to turn around and direct me further into his office. The office much like the man was nothing like I had expected.

"Wow. I have to say this is impressive. I love your space."

What I had guessed was his waiting area looked more like a den. Above the fireplace was a 50- inch flat screen fixed to the wall accompanied by a reclining sofa set and ottoman. The area was dimly lit with incents burning in the far corner of the room and a small rock waterfall that created the calmest sounds. I felt the warmth of his hand on my elbow and immediately turned my attention back to him.

"I'm happy you like it. Not too many people take the time to appreciate their atmosphere."

"Well one thing's for sure and two for certain it definitely beats my office if I could even call it that."

I tailed him and admired his office decorum until we reached his therapy room.

"Yeah I've gotten that reaction a few times. I actually like this place better than my last office. I hate when my clients don't feel like they're at home, so I decided to make my office just that. Don't get me wrong the professional building was ok, but for some reason the people that needed my attention still didn't feel like they could open up to me the way they needed or wanted to. So, I wanted to create a home away from home."

"Oh ok. I guess I can see your vision."

He laughed at my silent sarcasm but knew what I was saying was very true. As we made our way down the hall, I saw that he had two different therapy rooms. The one we were in was clearly for his women clients because it was decorated with all the things women love; fluffy rugs and flowers. The second room was the ideal man cave; TV that swallowed the wall, gaming chairs and a mini fridge. I guess the expression on my face said it all as I sat on the chaise.

"I'm sorry is this a little too informal for you?"

"Oh no not at all, I love it actually."

"Ok, well just let me know because the last thing I want is for you to be uncomfortable."

Listening to the way he spoke made me wonder if I sounded the same way to my clients. Not that there was anything wrong with how he spoke, but I found myself questioning just how genuine he was. I watched him shuffle through paperwork and could see how unprepared he was.

"Looks like good help is hard to come by too."

"Oh, you noticed that too huh? Yeah that's what happens when you fall in love with the help."

I couldn't suppress my laugh.

"That's funny?"

"Hilarious. But it's ok. I just hope I'm not on the clock yet."

"Laugh at my pain why don't you."

I didn't realize how serious he really was until he sat across from me and still hadn't cracked a smile.

"You're serious…I'm so sorry. I honestly thought you were joking."

"Nope."

"Well it's a good thing I'm allergic to love but have a great personality."
My sarcastic joke fell on deaf ears. Instead of laughing or even giving the impression that he was amused by my humor, he handed me the typical office paperwork with the required information highlighted. In turn, I quietly filled in the blanks and signed all the necessary documents before handing it back for his inspection. With a nod of the head he said,
"I'm sorry I didn't formally introduce myself... I'm Dr. Isaac or if you prefer you can call me Joseph."
He extended his hand and I obliged.
"Dr. Trinity Smith or just Trinity whichever you prefer."
"I'm sorry you said Dr. Trinity? What field."
I knew the question was coming and had prepared myself for the confusion the best I could.
"Psychology."
"Psychology? Wait I'm confused. Is this some kind of joke?"
"Nope. Look this is going to be as weird for me as it is for you. At the end of the day we're both human and while we dissect other people's problems and help them

reach a positive and peaceful solution, we still have problems of our own. Who should doctors turn to when they're in need?"

"Wow...well Dr. Trinity, you mind if I lay down?"

"So now you have jokes?"

"Yeah, these chaises are comfortable and looks like we both about to get some therapy in."

I laughed to myself,

"Well, be my guest. It's your office..."

He returned with a laugh of his own.

"After you.."

His playfulness made it easy for me to loosen up. I decided to move from the chaise to the round spinning chair.

"You don't like the chaise?"

"No, its cool but I love these chairs. Been thinking about getting one for my room."

Naturally I sat in the chair, kicked my shoes off and put my feet up.

"Good you're comfortable now we can get started."

In typical therapy fashion, he reached down on the floor to hit the record button on his voice recorder, but I stopped him.

"I know that recording sessions is what we typically do, but I'm requesting that our sessions be off the record. I'm not really looking for a resolution per say but more reassurance and comfort."

"Ok. I respect that."

"Thank you."

Picking the recorder up, he walked over to his desk and placed it in the desk drawer.

"So, tell me why you're here?"

Those wouldn't have been my choice of words to build a rapport, but to each his own.

"Because a really good friend of mine said and I quote that I needed to get help because giving it wasn't enough."

He laughed.

"That's funny to you?"

I mimicked him.

"Ha ha. I'm saying, what a harsh friend you have."

"I wouldn't call it harsh but real. We have a mutual respect for each other and he disagrees with the direction I've opted to take my career. He also knows a lot about me so he was saying it more out of concern than trying to be malicious."

"Care to share."

"Uhhhh…well I prefer to start at the beginning so you'll know the why before the what."

"I'm listening."

Rather than beating around the bush, I told him about my dreams. About my mother leaving and my dad's worsening depression at her absence. The random women that came and went. My longing for one of them to be able to be the woman figure my mother was to me for the time that I had her. The many disappointments and how they led to my wanting to start a career as a love surrogate.

"Do you think she loved you?"

"I don't know. I mean yes but her action says otherwise. I mean she would tell me all the time but hell I told half the men I dated I loved them and really didn't mean it. Not that I didn't want to, but I just didn't."

"And you're convinced that this would be helpful to men why?"

"Because after watching my father bring different women in and out of our lives, I realized that it wasn't about love…or however he really felt about them. It was more so about what they did for him…what void he needed filled at the time. That's where his happiness came from. I just want to be the one to fill the void…make them feel complete so that it won't be so hard for the next woman that comes along."

He laughed hysterically. I sat in silence looking at him sternly. Once he caught a glimpse that I was serious, he stopped.

"My apologies. That was very unprofessional of me."

"Very."

"I got a little too comfortable. Back to what you were saying."

"I'm done."

"Well do you mind if I give you my opinion."

With my arms crossed in front of my chest I nodded.

"Coming from a man that's had his fair share of ups with more downs, the only way to truly fill a void is with pure genuine love." This wasn't the first time I heard this nonsense, but I chose to entertain his thought.

"You're kidding me, right?"

I mimicked him in my school girl voice.

"...Pure genuine love."

"Why is love such a joke to you?"

"Because it doesn't exist! Hell, it doesn't even have a real concrete definition. The only thing definite about love is that it's an emotion. And everybody knows that emotions change with moods and moods change with people and people...people are imperfect so..."

I looked over at him and saw what looked like discernment in his eyes. Only I knew his search would be blank.

"Your rationality is… sad. Like you really believe that love can be replaced by temporary satisfaction."

"No…I believe that everyone… man and woman alike have their own agendas and love or lack there of is a distraction of truth. Like people claim to love someone but then say they hate or dislike things about that person. Then how can you say you love them then? Isn't love accepting a person as they are?"

"For someone who doesn't believe love is real you sure do have a strong take on it."

"I have to…"

The strength of my words faded. One thing about me that would always be misunderstood by my counterparts is my view of love. It's not a lack of belief or empty desire of want, just that my faith is well…null and void to the subject.

"Last I checked people only study things that spark their interest."

"Or…they do their research to make themselves aware, so they know what to avoid."

"Got to stay woke huh?"

"At all times."
We both sat in silence until it was interrupted by the sweet chime of his timer located on the corner of his desk. I looked down at my watch and realized our session was almost over.

"Wow time went by kind of quick."

"Yeah it does when you're engaged in a good conversation. So, will I see you same time next week?"

I hesitated. I thought about the client that I had just picked up here and how I could possibly seek help while trying to give it at the same time. This was only supposed to be a quick trip to relieve my mind. He sensed my hesitation.

"Next visit on me."

I had to be honest with myself, nothing sounded better than free. Plus, I still had a few things on my mind.

"Well if that's the case it would be rude of me not to accept. Guess next time, I'll give you the chance to vent a little."

He laughed.

"Sounds like a plan. Well Trinity,"

He stood up and helped me off the chair. I didn't realize just how tall he was until his 6'3" or 4" inch frame towered over me. I slid my shoes back on and accepted his hand.

"Same time?"

"Same place."

"Cool."

He showed me to the door and stood in the frame after I exited, watching me get into my car and start the engine. Right as I pulled away, I saw the door of his office close. I wouldn't say that today's session was as productive as I wished it would have been but everything about his vibe made it easy to get off subject. Since I was getting a buy one get one, I figured next session I would definitely stay on task and get to the real root of my problem. Pulling up to my temporary safe haven, I called my client to see if we could sit down for drinks and go over the events for the next couple of months. He confirmed. Instead of going in, I made a u-turn and headed for the closest market. Time to make this place feel like home.

****

The country girl in me slid across the hardwood floors in my stockings singing along to *Tennessee Whiskey*. I loved the lyrics and tone in his voice. It reminded me of my dad. How whenever he was in a good mood, I could climb into his lap while he watched tv and hum whatever song came to mind. His voice was amazing. He was my cinnamon kissed candy. I slid back across the floors and into the kitchen to pour myself another glass of wine. Bumping into the counter, my phone chimed. It was a message from Fabian. Reluctant to read it I did anyway.

> *Trinity. I hope all is well with you. I don't know what I did to make you ignore me these last few days, but I'm starting to get the hint. I want the best for you as you did for me. With that being said I would like for you to know that I have found someone that I have taken interest in. I just need your help in making sure that I'm not making a horrible mistake. She's nothing like you and I shared with you on several occasions that you are the type of woman I can see myself with for life. Though I know that's not possible, I just pray that you could extend a small portion of advice to me in this matter.*

> *Again, I thank you for all that you have done for me and pray that you will be blessed.*

Because Fabian sounded genuinely desperate, I entertained him.

> *Fabian. What a pleasure hearing from you and knowing that you have taken the necessary step to healing. I'm flattered that you still seek my help in this process and I'm more than willing to help.*
> *It's fairly simple though. You're incapable of making a mistake because you are seeking who can make you happy. Refer back to what you wrote on the card*
> *I AM SECURE BECAUSE…*
> *I believe it was something along the lines of you taking control and being a risk taker. We both know that you are so just live it. One day at a time. She may surprise you if you give her the fair chance she deserves.*

Immediately after pushing the send button, my phone rang. I hated that I typed all that only for him to call and interrupt what could have been a beautiful moment.

"Hello."

"It's good to hear your voice."

I smiled to myself although I was a bit annoyed.

"I just finished up my message to you."

"Well no need for that now."

"No. I literally just sent it and I'm currently wrapping up somethings for a client. I'll have to get in touch with you some other time."

"Wow. Just like that. You act as though we didn't have anything Trinity."

"Fabian. We agreed and you said that you understood that what happened between us was a mere simulation of what you needed to move on. Now I understand how our emotions felt a little more realistic than they were supposed to, but I was only doing what I was hired to do."

"You're right. My apologies."

"We're still friends so keep the apology. I'll talk to you soon ok?"

"Ok."

We disconnected the line. It was hard for me to say the things I said but I meant every word. I was only doing what I was hired to do, or at least that's what I convinced myself was true. My entire mood had changed. Walking over to the couch I plopped down and channel surfed until I dozed off anticipating what tomorrow would bring.

****

I woke up feeling refreshed. No bad dreams or hard feelings. On days like this, I just wanted to hit the mall. Not necessarily to shop but, I deserved a new pair of shoes and maybe a few outfits to add to my already ridiculous wardrobe. Figured I could kill 2 birds with one stone. Do a little of what I love and handle a little business at the same time. I didn't think it was too early for drinks so I called Clifton to see if he would be cool with doing brunch. Once I got the green light, I showered and hit the strip.

Walking into the mall, I felt like a child entering an amusement park for the first time. It was the type of excitement that caused a tickle in my stomach that ended with a grin on my face. I loved to people watch. There was something about watching peoples' actions and expressions that in many ways gave me life. There's so much you can learn about a person by just watching the way they walk or speak, their gestures, the way they react around a large or small group of strangers. I was home. To avoid looking like the weirdo in the middle of the mall starring at random spectators, I walked amongst the crowd and into a department store. For nothing in particular I browsed the racks. Looking up a few times, I saw a young couple that immediately held my attention. The short sundress she wore hugged her body perfectly as he towered over her. I watched her select several items for him and the way his facial expressions changed with approval or disapproval of her taste. They weaved amongst the racks of clothing. It was almost as if they were moving in slow motion. He followed close behind her until she stopped at a display of button-down shirts. Fingering the shirts, he bent down and licked the tip of her ear. She jumped slightly at his affection and closed her eyes biting her lip gently. He proceeded and sensually kissed her neck. She welcomed his kisses, leaning her head oh so slightly in the opposite direction. With closed eyes, she reached behind her and found his now protruding girth. Caressing him through his pants, he in turn lifted the flow of her dress and allowed his hands to explore the inner gap of her thighs…

"Trinity!"

My trance was broken by a familiar voice. I turned and faced him.

"Hey Joseph."

Shocked I looked back at the couple who were now facing the back wall looking through the shirts that hung from it. Confused I turned back to Joseph.

"You like what you see?"

I was slow to respond because apparently my mind had been playing tricks on me.

"Yeah I was looking at those shirts over there."

He smirked to himself.

"Really, which one?"

He proceeded to walk around me and in the direction of where my daydream started. I tailed behind him. Once we stood in the very spot where I watched the two lovers display their feelings for one another he spoke again.

"This one? I really think it'll fit you quite nice."

I playfully nudged him.

"Shut up! How long were you standing there?"

"Long enough to know that something had your attention and it wasn't this hideous shirt. What were you thinking about?"
As bad as I wanted to lie, I couldn't.

"I was watching the couple that was just over here."

"That much I figured but they weren't doing anything out of the norm which is why I don't understand why it took me saying your name directly in your ear to get your attention."

"Have you ever just sat back and watched how people interact with each other? Like that couple for instance. Just putting yourself in their shoes?"

"Fantasizing about being in love like they are?"

"No! You don't know that they're in love."

"You don't know that they're not. Let's go ask them."
I grabbed his arm.

"Are you crazy? Leave them alone and let them be."
He laughed to himself.

"You were the one over there starring at them and daydreaming."

"Yeah whatever."
I looked up at him and saw that he was looking at me with lust in his eyes.

"Why are you looking at me like that?"

"Like what?"

Rather than entertain him or take a chance of my mind getting the best of me yet again I suggested we grab a bite to eat.

"Hungry?"

"I can eat."

"Would you like to get something here or somewhere else?"

"Well they have a pretty nice selection here and around the food court. That way you can feed your body and your mind."

"My mind?"

"Yeah. Give yourself the chance to finish people watching and daydream a little longer."

I rolled my eyes but there was truth in his statement.

"Yeah you're right."

"Cool. There's a little Italian place here I like. I think you will to. Come on…my treat."

"But I asked you."

"True but the man in me won't let you, so come on."

Walking out of the store, my phone buzzed in the bottom of my bag, it was Clifton. I hadn't mentioned to Joseph that I has already began my 'hands-on' practice and was supposed to be meeting my client.

Something in me wouldn't let me. Instead I hit the ignore button and sent a quick text 'Cancel today, talk later.' Rather than him texting back, he called again.

"You need to get that?"

"No. it's a client. I can return their call later."

"You sure?"

"Positive."

Walking to the restaurant we made small talk about our careers. What made us enter the field and how we enjoy and hate helping people. Once we got to our table, the conversation became more personal.

"Our stories are kind of similar, but I grew up without my mother and father. My grandmother raised me. And to this very day if my mother came back, I would welcome her with open arms."

"She left you with her mother?"

"No, my dad's mom."

"Wow. That's different."

"Yeah it is. My maternal grandmother was into drugs and my dad was killed when I was a baby. My grandmother refuses to tell me how I ended up in her care, but she never spoke an ill word about my mother. When I was little, I used to sit on her porch with flowers, waiting for her to come and she never said anything."

He laughed a sorrowful laugh.

"Not even about me picking the fresh flowers that she planted. She would just go and get more. I guess me picking them gave her a reason to work in her garden on the regular. I would wrap them up and put a bow around them. She would look at me, shake her head and keep doing whatever she was doing."

Listening to him speak made my eyes water but I refused to cry or let him see the tears form in the bottom of my eyes. I just looked away as he spoke.

"I'm sorry if I'm talking too much."

"Uhhh…Joseph it's what we do. There's no such thing. It actually feels good to hear you talk about your past…actually makes it a little easier for me to want to talk about mine."

"I have to admit it does. Like you said when you came to my office, who do we have to turn to when we need to release?"

"Exactly."

The waitress walked up beside us and placed plates in front of us.

"Umm excuse me.."

Before I could tell the waitress that we hadn't placed our order yet, he stopped me.

"I ordered before we got here. I told you I love this place. I just ordered us the same thing."

"Oh..ok well thank you."

Soon after she walked away, another waiter walked up with a bottle of wine in hand with 2 glasses. Despite the fact we were in the mall, I started to feel the atmosphere change and become more intimate. Sipping my wine, Joseph and I talked for what seemed like hours. We laughed to the point of tears and embraced hands through the tales of our pain. I didn't want this moment to end. Immediately I felt nauseated. My brain was telling me that my emotions and feelings of endearment were at levels my mind could not withstand.

"Well, this was healthy."

"Huh?"

"Our talk. It's about time we get out of here don't you think?"

A look of confusion engulfed his face. He looked down at his watch and responded with disappointment.

"Yeah I guess it is. Been here longer than expected. You want to go back to my office? Talk some more?"

Deep down I wanted to say yes but the knots forming in my stomach answered for me.

"I'm good. We can pick up where we left off next week at my session."
With a small nod of the head he flagged the waitress to bring the check.

"Sounds like a plan. So, what you got going this evening if you don't mind me asking."
I really didn't have anything planned minus rescheduling with Clifton but still wasn't ready to tell Joseph my other focus while I was here.

"Oh, I'll probably call my client back and just chill. Get some real valuable me time."

"OK, Ok. That's cool I can dig that."
Getting up from the table he pulled my chair out and assisted me with standing. He offered his arm and reluctantly I accepted. We walked this way until we reached the escalator. Behind us were a couple of teenagers.

"Damn she fine."

"Dude you just gone say that about this man wife in front of him? Look, if he turns around and smack you don't expect me to help, I'm telling you that now."

"Shut up with your scary ass."

I decided to entertain them.

"Thank you but watch your mouth. A gentleman watches his language in front of a lady."

"Oh yes ma'am. I am so sorry. Let me introduce myself..."

Joseph turned around.

"How about you don't and say you did." I looked at him and he winked at me playfully.

"Oh, my bad sir just giving credit where credit is due, but you need to watch your wife, she's hitting on me."

I couldn't hold my laugh.

"Excuse me little boy."

"Oh, that's Mr. Little boy to you. Coming around here looking like that. You know us young boys can't control our hormones."

He nudged his friend in the arm.

"Man speak for yourself. I got this. You the one that want other men's women."

"We're..."

Before I could finish my sentence, Joseph interjected.

"Good. Thank you lil homie. Y'all have fun and stay out of trouble."

"Oh, bet we gone do that."

Once we reached the bottom floor, Joseph took my hand in his and we proceeded to the garage.

"Why did you do that."

"Just giving the kids a show that's all."

"Yeah right."

"Where did you park?"

Looking around the garage, I hit the button to my rental and waited for the alarm to go off.

"Are you serious?"

"Hey it works."

We laughed and walked in the direction of the loud echoes of my panic switch. Once we were close enough, I silenced it.

"Well if you change your mind and want to get out just let me know. I don't have anything planned for today."

"Ok, I will."

I lied. I didn't have any intentions on contacting him again unless it was for therapy. The feeling that came over me as we talked was oh too familiar and even though it wasn't a bad thing, it definitely wasn't a feeling I needed right now. Not with me trying to establish myself as a Love surrogate to broken men. I was beginning to like Joseph and nothing about that was healthy for me.

"See you…Thursday right?"
He stood in silence for a minute.
"Yeah, see you Thursday."
Once I was tucked away in the car, I pulled my phone out of my purse and saw several missed calls from Clifton. I tried calling him back, but my calls were being sent to voicemail. Once I made it back to my living space, I sent him a text.

> *Me: Hey I'm sorry about today. I got a little caught up and was unable to get away. Call me when you get this.*

I figured since he wasn't responding to my calls, it would take him a minute to respond to my text which was surprisingly untrue. He responded almost immediately.

> *Clifton: No apologies. But I have decided that I'm not going to need your services.*
> *Looks like you already have a client and all the things you said to me were false. Thanks anyway and the best to you both. Oh, and don't worry about the deposit its yours.*

I was in shock. Apparently, he saw Joseph and I together and made the assumption that he was a client. I really didn't know how to respond but opted to respect his decision even though it set me back both mentally and financially.

> *Me: What you saw was not what you thought I can assure you, but if you are certain that you don't want my services then I have no choice than to respect your decision. If you change your mind, you know how to reach me. Keep in mind I'm only here temporarily. Hope to hear from you soon.*

I figured that he wouldn't respond so I went to the kitchen grabbed a glass and poured up. When plans change, I simply regroup and reform. With a wine glass in one hand and my phone in the other, it was time to move on to the next client. I thought about Camden's demand that I just come back home but something held me here. Opening

my POF profile, my stomach dropped when
his face popped up in my inbox.

****

   "Good morning."

   "Morning."

I felt strange knowing my "secret" was
somewhat exposed.

   "You good?"

Apparently, my thoughts had become
sleeves on my sleeveless sundress. I
opted to fake the funk.

   "Great. You? You alright?"

He smiled.

   "Couldn't be better."

The conversation between us was more
awkward than 2 strangers waking up
together after a night of drunk sex that
neither of them remembered.

   "You know what…"

We spoke simultaneously and laughed in
sync. Being a gentleman, he offered me to
speak first.

   "My bad. You first."

   "Is it me or does today just
seem…awkward?"

Shrugging his shoulders, he twisted his lips
somewhat, not confirming or denying my

statement. Instead he answered my question with a question.

"Why you say that? You feel awkward being here?"

Playing coy I ignored his question and asked another.

"What were you going to say?"

He sensed that I was detouring the conversation and unlike the back and forth question battle I was expecting, he answered with no hesitation.

"I was going to suggest we chill in the mancave but seems to me like you have something else on your mind."

I didn't know whether his was playing dumb to get info out of me or if he was being truly genuine until he asked,

"You have something you want to tell me?"

I looked around dumbfounded but really was contemplating on telling him the truth. Not that I wanted to lie but I didn't feel the need to explain my actions or tactics.

"So…"

"So what?"

"Trinity, I know it's your profile. Your non-response to my message confirmed that."

"No shit Sherlock. But what do you want me to say about it. My profile description is pretty self-explanatory."
Then it dawned on me.

"Wait. You don't think I'm on there to date, do you?"
I had offended him with my question without intending to.

"I'm sorry…I didn't mean it…"
He smirked.

"Some happen to find love in the lamest places I guess."

"I really wasn't…"
He cut my apology short yet again. This time walking to the therapy room. I hesitantly followed. Rather than letting our past intro linger he changed the subject and got right to business.

"So, since you don't believe in true love for yourself, what makes you think you're capable of restoring the aspects of love in your clients."

"I'd like to compare my thoughts about love to the concept of Santa. Santa isn't real per say but because we are taught as kids that he is and the other kids around us were taught the same thing, we didn't have a reason to believe he wasn't. That is until we

grew up and started questioning and making sense of things on our own."
I sat down and kicked my feet up with confidence.

"Joseph, I don't care how many different ways you ask me the same question nothing is going to change about the way I feel."
He looked at me helplessly.

"To be honest, I didn't come here looking for a solution or answer as to why I don't believe in love or why I've decided to take the hands-on approach with male clients that prefer this method, I'm here to vent and find a different coping method of dealing with losing my mother."

"So you don't think one has anything to do with the other?"

"Maybe…"
He sat silent. His quiet demeanor bothered me. The longer we sat in silence the more my thoughts ran endlessly through my head. I questioned myself again. 'Why am I here'. With each thought his facial expression changed. Finally, he spoke.

"Why are you running?"
Before I could fully digest his question and bottle my aggravation, the chime of his front door sang.

"Give me a sec and think about it."

Before I had the chance to excuse myself from the room, he brushed past me and went to the front. Rather than contesting me staying and finishing the conversation, I sat back against the chair and gazed at the ceiling. My being here was no mistake. Coming from a man that's had his fair share of ups with more downs… his words rippled through my mind. Swiveling around in the chair until I was facing the door, I could see what appeared to be the silhouette of a woman. Their voices were mumbled but the conversation seemed intense. Was now my chance to prove to him that my services as a love surrogate are not as ridiculous as they seem? The more I thought about it the closer I moved to the door before I even realized that I was visible to them. She looked at me as if I was wearing the scarlet letter and I looked through her as if she were glass. Fighting through fear and embarrassment, I went to his aid.

"Is everything ok?"

"Yes. Everything is fine…Ms. Vance was just leaving."

"And who are you? Let me guess the new assistant."

Her attitude and sarcasm carried a fragrance that was far from welcoming and before he had the chance to respond I flooded her negativity with my scent.

"Assistant? No possible partner, Dr. Trinity Smith."

I knew using the word partner would leave her guessing as to what my real position was. It also gave me the time I needed to create whatever atmosphere I wanted to create with Joseph; however, the absence of my extended hand in our introduction was clear.

"Trinity, this really isn't necessary."

"First name basis already I see."

Her words fell on deaf ears.

"Well maybe you and I will get there as well one day."

"Oh, that'll never happen."

"Trinity…"

"On second thought Dr. Isaac, you and I co-existing in your establishment is a perfect idea. You could use the help and I'm willing to assist wherever you see fit. I'll let you finish up here and we can discuss the details later."

I brushed my hand across his elbow in my passing while looking her in the eyes. Walking back into the therapy room, I gathered my things and passed between them. Turning to face his past,

"It was a pleasure meeting you. Ms. Vance, right?"

She ignored my petty remark with a childish antic of her own; turning her head with her nose in the air. I chuckled to myself then turned to face Joseph.

"We'll be in touch."

I winked seductively. I could see the hurt and frustration in his eyes.

"Trinity."

"Talk to you soon."

His scent was intoxicating. From this point forward, I was his and he was mine. No more running, only I couldn't give him exactly what he wanted but I could pretend to be all that he needed. Day one with Mr. Needy.

****

Entering the condo, I dropped everything on the counter and went straight for the bottle. Wine was my serum. I needed to think. I myself could never be involved with a man so needy but he looked like he was about to drown and seeing as he was contacted to be my help, I couldn't just stand by and watch. He was handsome true but ultimately, a needy man is the ultimate turn off. I walked into the living room and grabbed my laptop.

Mr. Needy
36 yr old male
Psychiatrist

Before I could complete my list of KNOWS about Joseph, there was a knock at the door. I sat quiet for a minute because no one knew I was here. I figured maybe it was someone looking for an old resident or some kids running from door to door until they knocked again. Hesitantly, I got up from my spot on the couch and looked through the peep hole. Slowly I opened the door.

"Joseph, how did you know…"
He kissed me before I could complete my sentence. Shocked by it all, I allowed it to happen. I welcomed his tongue and he did the same with mine. His lips were soft yet strong. The intensity behind his emotional connection with me was frightening. I pulled away.

"Fix me."
Caught off guard, my emotions scrambled. I had set the bait but didn't expect the catch. Not only that, I really didn't have a legit plan behind what I was going to do to help but at

this moment I had a point to prove. Men need women in many ways and he too would become a believer in everything outside of love.

"Are you sure?"

With his forehead pushed into mine he nodded and allowed his lips to meet mine again. The tingle between my legs was intense this time and I couldn't escape him. He picked me up and used my feet to close the door. Laying me on the couch, his body mass covered me, and I removed his shirt. This isn't how I had hoped to begin our situationship, but it's what we both needed. Our connection was different from Fabian and I. He reminded me so much of Camden it was scary. With each thrust of his hips into mine I felt my veins melt, each muscle relaxed and each thought fade into empty memories of what I wished to say. His sex faces spoke to me in a strange way. They whispered comfort into my ears, security over my head, and pleasure throughout my limbs. With each moan he transferred more of his energy into me. My fear of this man became my will to please him. It was my turn to provide comfort, security, and pleasure to ease his needy nature. I would convince him that he doesn't need anyone to make him relevant but that they need him to grow on their own. With the completion of that thought, he emerged from inside of me and caught his legacy in his hands. I tried to stand so that I could assist with cleaning, but his expression told me to stay still and I did. I laid back down and waited for him to return. I anticipated an encore but that's not what he had in mind. He laid on top of me, this time with his long frame extended beyond the length of the sofa, resting his head on my now bare chest. Naturally I caressed him. Running my fingers through his hair he let out a sorrowful sigh. I felt the tears leave his eyes and connect with my skin. Rather than ask the obvious or quote the generic words of comfort, I said what I wanted to hear.

"She's gone and it's ok to accept that."

For years I knew how hard it was to hold on to the thought of my mother returning. Sad to say that it felt good meeting someone with the same restriction but there's nothing like feeling alone. Feeling like you need that one person to make you complete until you realize that you may never be. It's the reason I dreamed of her so often and the reason he felt it necessary to see, hear and feel a woman next to him despite how good or bad she may be.

****

We went on dates here and there. Each one felt more and more intimate. We became partners and counseled couples that longed for answers or refused to give up hope in their hopeless situations. He was the romantic and I was the realist. He made them dream and I made them accept the outcome...good or bad. I reorganized his entire office and taught him how to be self-sufficient. His ex was smart. I had no choice but to give her that much credit. She managed to come into his office and set up shop right under his nose. She created a system that she thought only she knew how to run and made it so that he had no choice but to depend on her. So much so she was able to not only steal money from him but cheat on him with a few of his clients. I figured she got caught up and a little sloppy with her dirt and that's how things ended between her and Joseph, but I chose to keep my assumptions or as I would like to call it my concluded thesis to myself.

Fixing him was hard because we built a bond so early on. It wasn't either of our intentions but was something that could not be ignored nor denied. It was as if the bond wasn't new but much like the one I have with someone else. Their personalities, physic, even bad habits matched to a T. I caught myself thinking about him from time to time but immediately shook the thoughts of Camden and I. I enjoyed Joseph's company and he enjoyed mine, but this wasn't about us, it was about him learning to be on his own. We agreed that for every date we went on together, he would also go on one alone. We also agreed that we could no longer be intimate; well I vowed to myself that I could not be intimate with him and he respected my decision. This particular night made him hard to resist. Being the corny, coy woman that I am I enjoy things like walks on the beach and picnics. Knowing this, Joseph arranged for us to meet and watch a movie under the stars with other spectators. I was hesitant at first but was coaxed into laying in his arms while we lay amongst the crowd.

"Pass me the backpack."

I grabbed the backpack and before giving it to him decided to take a peek inside,.

"Dang nosey. I said pass it to me."

"Yeah whatever."
I dug into the bag and pulled out an apple juice.

"For me? You are too sweet."

"Yeah whatever…"
He mimicked me. I laughed then rested my chin on his shoulder.

"So, buddy… what we watching?"
He shushed me and pointed at the screen. O. The classic remake of Othello. I loved this movie and how it was full of fake yet the real depiction love. I remember the first time I saw the film, it made me want to test the depths of my own emotions with the possibility of reaching what I had given up on. Being here did something to me. Not wanting to accept the fact that I'm a woman with needs just like the next, I forgot what that felt like. Every so often I found myself looking at him out of the corner of my eye. A few times I caught him doing the same.

"You want some of my apple juice?"
I offered my straw to him to take a sip before pulling it back teasing.

"Ok, keep playing."

"Or what?"
His eyes were captivating.

"You know this aint what you want Trinity."

"Aint nobody scared of you."

"Good. Because I don't want you to be." Without fair warning he leaned in and kissed me. The tingle between my legs was intense and before I had the chance to see if his reaction matched mine, we were interrupted by a bright light; the officer stood over us.

"Excuse me fine couple, I'm going to have to ask you two to keep your lovin' to a minimum."

"Our apologies officer."

"None needed. Enjoy the movie." As he walked away, we exploded in laughter. Laying his head in my lap, I stroked his head all the while thinking. I can't possibly start falling, now is not the time I have a job to do.

"Just relax, we both know what this is. I respect that I can't have you, but I just need you a little while longer." I hated how he could read my mind at any given time.

"Shut up."

I tried to play it off, but my heart wouldn't let go of how this moment felt. I turned the hourglass in my head, and it was time to make a move.

****

So, what you're saying is that it's possible to love 2 people at the same time?"

"You love both your parents, don't you?"

"Trinity, now's not the time…be a little more open minded please?"

I glared at Joseph and was cold to his remark. I couldn't respond the way I wanted to because we were in the middle of a heated therapy session with one of our couple clients, but he knew he was definitely in for a tongue lashing when the timer sounded.

"Kathy, listen please. He loves you. And he's in love with you or he wouldn't have asked you to be his wife. He wouldn't have felt the need to be so open with you if he didn't really and truly want to be with you for the rest of his life. But yes, it is possible to love more than one person just not be in love with them. I think that's what Dr. Trinity was getting at."

I glared over at Joseph again. The little black woman crawled onto my shoulder and screamed

I know like hell this man didn't just twist my words to appease her. No sister you dumb as hell if you

> *marry a man that is telling you to*
> *your face that he loves you and*
> *his female best friend equally.*

My sarcasm was strong and why Joseph was trying to play with my emotions and theirs was beside me, but the last few weeks between us were awkward. Unlike Fabian, I didn't feel his connection to me growing. Something in me liked when they didn't want the process to end but Joseph seemed to be rushing the process along. After our date at the park, I reached out to him on several occasions to hang out and he was already engaged in something. Our outside meetings became less and less frequent and I started looking forward to the couple therapy sessions just to be around him but even the sessions weren't the same. Now definitely wasn't the time for me to get in my emotions, but I couldn't control myself. It was me that said that I couldn't allow myself to feel for my clients. That I had an objective. Heal and help; make money and move. I let Joseph control the rest of the sessions and contributed a dry he's right here and there until their time expired. Without a word I joined him in escorting our clients out and immediately went for my things.

"What's your issue?"

"Nothing. We don't have any other sessions, so I'm headed home."

He grabbed my arm and forced me to face him.

"We were a simulation remember. I can't have you because we're nothing but a mere simulation to fix whatever issue you think it is I have."

"Think? NO! I know you have. But I'm happy to see that you've been able to make progress on your own. You're not as needy as you used to be when I first met you."

"Needy?"

"Yes. Needy. You lost your mother at a young age, so you yearned the company of a woman, any woman to just fill the void rather than just living your life freely. If you can't move around without the company of a woman you won't move around. But you don't have that issue anymore. We don't hang out anymore and whenever I reach out to you, you're already out and about… Mission complete."

He stood quiet for a moment.

"Did it ever occur to you that I just don't like doing things alone?"

"It did until I analyzed the fact that one, you don't have very many male friends and two, the majority of the things you like to do work out better when you're with someone of the opposite sex."

Again, he was quiet.

"Look, I'm in my feelings because I thought this process was going to take a little longer and I was actually starting to feel something but I'm thankful that you brought me back to earth. So, if you will excuse me, I have a bottle of wine waiting for me."

He stepped to the side and allowed me to finish gathering my things. Once I got back to the door I spoke dramatically over my shoulder.

"This isn't goodbye, just a see you later." I didn't give him a chance to speak. Either he was going to follow behind me with a series of questions, or just let me leave. It didn't matter either way because what little work I needed to do was done and money was made on both our behalves.

Once I made it back to the condo, I poured myself glass after glass of wine. With each pour came more doubt.

"Love Surrogate."

I spoke out loud and laughed to myself. I didn't think that I would find myself liking any of the men I encountered, but there had to be some type of chemistry on both ends in order for it really work. As my mind wandered, my hands packed. Over the past few months I had acquired a nice new wardrobe and a few new knickknacks to bring back home with me. Flying was definitely out of the question, so I called for a one-way rental, and prepared myself for the 4 hour drive back to the city I called home, Houston.

Somewhere between glasses and packing, I fell asleep on the couch. Blind searching for my phone, I felt his hand on my back. His live touch startled me,

"You ok?"

I realized I was half dressed but he was fully clothed, so I made the safe assumption that nothing happened.

"When…"

"Been here. You texted me…remember?"

"Clearly not. I was drinking and packing. That's all I recall."

Looking at my phone, I saw the story of a message I sent to Joseph which explained why he was here.

"You know it's not too late to allow yourself to feel anything Trinity."

"I beg to differ. Wow. I really need to stop drinking."

"No, you really need to stop running."

"I'm not running. I'm a realist amongst dreamers, big difference."

"Right. Is that why you had a whole attitude about me growing and not being quote unquote needy? Just admit it Trinity…you have love for me and don't want to let it go."

"Love? Boy stop. Lust maybe…but not love."

"Oh really?"

"Yeah really."

I kissed him wildly and passionately. His hands traveled my body just as I wanted them too and despite the fact that I knew I was treading dangerous waters, I wanted this memory; I needed this memory. It was a solid goodbye and separation from another client. He took me in his mouth and kissed the lips between my legs just right. I moaned with each flick of his tongue until my breathing sped up and I was forced to release all the tension in my body. He sipped humbly and accepted my flavor. Getting up I escorted him into the bedroom where I consummated my emotions and our situationship.

<u>"Mr. Companionship"</u>

"My dude! So, you want to explain to me why you out here while the party is in there?"

"Dog look, I'm only here because your big day is tomorrow, and I have to be. Other than that, you know I would be at the crib chilling."

"That's the problem you always at the crib."

"Aint, nothing wrong with that."

"It is. Man, I'm tired of seeing my ace cooped up. You need to get out more."

"Nah. I'm straight."

"How?"

He spoke between taking sips of beer.

"How is being in the house, going to the gym and work straight?"

"Because I'm making and keeping money, staying healthy and avoiding chicken heads like that."

I pointed to the chick inside the party that kept eyeing me like I was the last link of sausage on the barbeque pit. I knew my boy only wanted the best for me, but I was done with all of it. Countless women came and went, and I opted not to keep any of them by choice. It wasn't that I didn't want a relationship, but not being in one at the moment was much easier.

"Nah my dude you still stuck on what's her name…"

"You bet not say it…"

He laughed at my pain, but the wound wasn't completely scabbed over.

"Man, whatever but I still think she out there waiting for you man. We are good brothers that deserve good women."

"Yeah ok."

On several occasions I went through this mini hiatus that sent my boys into a frenzy. I tried to convince them that there is nothing wrong with me being alone all the time and not wanting to hang, but they weren't having it. It was hard for me to tell them that I didn't want to hang out because I got tired of always being the only single in the mix, but I let it be known and when I did, instant regret. My boys tried to hopelessly set me up on blind dates but not one worked. It never failed that every last one of the women I met had issues. Not minor but major. But each time I agreed to go because as much as I hated to admit, I admired what my brothers had. Each of them found someone that they really and truly loved, and Tyson was the last of bunch, minus me.

"On some real talk bro, this is unhealthy. You need to find someone to really make you happy."

Again, he was right, but I didn't want him to see that I was with him 100%.

"Well I know one thing for sure."

"What's that?"

"I can't depend on you or them to hook me up."

We laughed.

"Well if you need a little help..."

"Nah dog I'm straight."

"But for real I got you."

"Yeah all the way messed up."

"Whatever. Man let's get back to the party. I saw a few of these chicks eyeballing you bro, you might get lucky."

Luck isn't exactly what I had in mind but wherever the ball rolled at this point I didn't care, I was tired of being lonely.

****

"Trinity..."

His voice lingered from a distance yet rang a sweet tune in my head as I sat on the park bench reading *'The Collective Autobiographies of Maya Angelou'*

"Trinity!"

I hadn't seen Camden in ages, so his presence made me feel like a school girl that yearned the attention of her crush. Looking at how the morning sun illuminated his broad shoulders and its dew created a soft glow off of his caramel mocha blended skin tone made me question how non-believers don't believe that men like this were truly made in the image of Jesus himself.

"So, you weren't gone call me and tell me you made it back in town."

"I didn't know you were still here."

"If you would have called you would have known."

"Oh whatever."

"Well?"

"Well what?"

"Girl get up off that bench and give me some love."

We shared a laugh. It was crazy that despite the fact we hadn't seen each other in almost a decade we could pick up a conversation as if time had never passed us. Just being there with him brought back memories from our childhood. I remember as a kid Camden always talked about how he was going to be this famous model that traveled the world to pick up women of all races to 'share his loving with' since I didn't want it. Well needless to say he stayed true to his word after his breakup that is.

"So how is this beautiful world and the women in it treating you?"
He squeezed me a little tighter after my comment. I melted in his arms and blended with his scent.

"Stop boy you stink."

"Yeah but you like it."
I pushed him away from me and returned to my seat on the bench. He picked up the sleeve to my favorite novel and read it aloud with a smirk on his face showing off the dimples I loved to hate. I slightly downed my head to quickly regain myself before I got lost in lust. I couldn't resist rubbing his muscular arms as he sat down next to me but retracted my touch after the moisture from his skin brought back a not so wanted emotion and memory. It wasn't that the feeling of his skin didn't excite me, but I didn't want him to know that I still felt that connection to him after all these years.

"Trinity, I'm serious. I miss you girl...excuse me woman. You're still as beautiful as the last time I saw you."
It bothered me that his compliments meant so much to me compared to the many other men I encountered.

"Oh, my goodness. Here you go!"

"Come on girl you know I love you."
And just like that my cool switch was turned off. The words 'I love you' echoed and bounced off my brain like screeching nails against a chalk board. I instantly morphed into a flat bellied reptile ready to retreat into my borough where I knew I would be safe. He sensed it.

"Lighten up. I'm just happy to see you."

"Same here."
He downed his head and licked his top lip as if he were deep in thought slowly tracing the font on my book's cover. He slowly lifted his head just enough for his eyes to catch a glimpse of heavens awakening.

"Brunch?"

"Yeah we can do that but let me stop by the crib shower and change first. Cool?"

"That's cool. Guess I'm following you then."
He helped me off the bench and we walked in the middle of the awkward silence that

wrapped itself tightly around us until we reached our cars. The entire time I followed him my mind raced. Thoughts of why I still felt so strongly about him and how bad I wanted to feel him inside of me flooded my brain; spilling through my veins until the desire rested between my legs. I knew that nothing was going to happen once we reached his place, but I would be lying if I said I didn't want it to. I parked my car next to his in the parking garage and followed him upstairs. My natural instinct lead me to grab his hand as we walked toward the elevator. He didn't deny my action, he embraced it as if our minds were connected and he expected it. Opening the door, I walked in behind him and followed him into the bathroom.

"Dang this is nice. When you move in here?"

He laughed.

"It is nice. Too bad it aint mine."

"Air bnb?"

"Yep. Now can you get out, so I can take a shower please?"

"Why? You don't have anything I haven't seen before."

"Dang ok momma!"

We shared a laugh. I sat on the toilet with my chin resting in my hands anticipating and ready for Camden to satisfy my curiosities with a show. But instead of getting undressed in front of me, he stepped into the shower behind the frosted glass and threw his clothes over the stall.

"Aww you're no fun."

"Nah you just nasty!"

"I know you are but what am I?"

He wiped a small circle on the shower door just enough to see me thru before he responded,

"Childish."

We both laughed again.

"So how much longer will you be in town?"

"About a week give or take a few days why?"

I didn't want him to think that I wanted to rekindle anything between us, but my car thoughts revisited me and I started to miss the way he felt. I mean the man was my first.

"No reason just asking."

"Nah you want something. You can't play me T, I know you."

"Whatever."

Rather than tell the truth about the tingle between my thighs, I opted to talk about my therapy sessions, leaving out a few major details.

"What…spit it out sexy lady. You want some of big daddy?"

His humor forced me to laugh. And much like Joseph he could read me on the drop of a hat, but he didn't need to know this.

"Shut up fool! No, I wanted to tell you about the therapy sessions."

"Oh yeah that's right. How did that go?"

"It went really well actually."

"Oh, for real. So, no more dreams?"

"Nope. That's crazy huh?"

"Not really especially since I been telling you to talk to somebody that may be able to help you cope."

If he only knew how well Joseph was able to help and hurt all at the same time.

"Well you were right ok. The therapist was able to put some other things on my mind too."

"Oh really? Like what?"

"Don't get it twisted I am completely and utterly satisfied with my life. Not having to deal with the same ole tired man on a permanent basis is working for me, but IF I do and I do mean IF the right one comes along, I will be capable of being the woman he needs."

"Well damn! You know how I feel about that. The right man has already come along but you have your eyes closed so tight its messing with the good brain cells you have left. But I'll admit, I'm proud of you. You took that first step…that's big of you T."

Stepping out of the shower, I couldn't resist myself any longer. I wrapped my arms around his neck and kissed his chest making sure to avoid his attempts to kiss my lips. Grabbing the back of my thighs, he lifted me effortlessly and sat me on the bathroom counter. I continued to put soft sensual kisses on his pecks allowing him to undress my lower half.

"T…"

His voice was faint.

Without a second thought he entered me, and I was immediately fulfilled. My body shivered with each thrust as I followed his rhythm.

"Trinity…"

His voice grew firmer as he sang my name and increased the intensity of his stroke. He laughed seductively in my ear.

"Trinity Michelle Smith."

My trance was broken.

"Damn girl you in here moaning and daydreaming. I told you if you want some of big daddy, I'm yours."

"Shut up I just had a moment."

"One that could last a lifetime if you stop being hard headed."

I rolled my eyes and wrapped my arms around his waist. He didn't reject my touch but didn't embrace me the way I had expected.

"When are you..."

I shushed him. He shook his head and held me. He tried to pull back and look at me, but I wouldn't let him. I couldn't. I needed a recharge but didn't want to complicate things. Being intimate with Camden would only complicate things more than I wanted to deal with right now. Finally, I pulled back,

"You ready yet? I'm starving."

He stood there looking at me dumbfounded.

"Trinity?"

I ignored him. I could feel his unspoken words creeping in my veins.

"I'll meet you in the car."

"Really? Ok Trin."

He brushed past me somewhat aggressively, grabbing his shirt and pulling it over his head.

"What's your problem?"

His glance was cold and blank

"Nothing. Let's roll."

Reaching for his arm, he turned away from me denying my advance and motioned for me to walk out the door as he held it open. I could sense he was annoyed and immediately I regretted my actions. He knew how I felt, and I knew how he felt but I couldn't stomach hearing him preach to me about how good of a man he could be to and for me. It's why I ignored his calls, messages and emails as often as I did for so long. I couldn't hold his heart and feared breaking it again. The elevator ride was dead silent. No more laughing, joking or playful girlfriend/boyfriend games. Just silence. Once we made it back to the cars, I opted to break the silence.

"So, am I riding with you or you riding with me?"

"Neither. You take your car and I'll take mine."

"How much sense does that make when we're going to the same place?"

He looked at me nonchalantly.

"Are you serious Cam? You really about to be this petty because we didn't…"

He cut my statement short.

"Fuck? Trinity get out yo feelings. If I wanted to, we would have. I'm the same dude that's been chasing a stubborn ass woman for years now. Stop it. I'm just sick of you acting like your feelings are the only ones that need to be heard and taken seriously. So, get in your car and follow me or don't I could really careless."

And there it was. Bottled emotions.

"Look I just wanted to…"

"Are you following me or not?"

My whole vibe had shifted and so did his. A part of me wanted to just go home, but the other part of me owed him the opportunity to vent.

"Guess I'm following you."

I had never seen this side of Cam. For the first time in a long time I felt like I wasn't in charge. The tone in his voice was chilling. I prayed that the trip to the restaurant would give both me and him the opportunity to calm and regroup. He pulled in first blocking 2 parking spots for us allowing me to park first. Once we were parked and seated, he didn't waste any time going in on me.

"So, you decided to pursue this little business idea of yours huh?"

"Do you have to say it like that? Hell, it was your idea!"

"I wasn't being serious Trinity and you know that."

"Well…"

"It's ridiculous."

"Whatever!"

I made sure my tone was nonchalant with a hint of 'I don't give a damn'. He laughed hysterically but his laughter struck me as insulting. I sat silently starring him in his eyes without blinking just to confirm just how serious I was about my career.

"You big mad or little mad?"

"None of the above. I happy with the money I'm making fixing broken men like you."

I really struck a nerve. Sorry not sorry. I felt attacked and struck back.

"Broken men like me…"

He spoke low with his head down. As bad as I wanted to offer an apology for my low blow, I couldn't muster one up.

"Wow. It's amazing how you play the clean-up woman behind women like you."

I was immediately on the defense.

"Excuse me?"

"Think about it…bi-polar women like you hurt men like me leaving us with insecurities, trust issues, and full of pain. Then here you come, back behind the same woman that caused the issue and try to "fix him" and restore what "they" took or created so that a real woman can get what she deserves. Really all you're doing is righting your own wrong."

"Women like me?"

"Yeah…you're the woman that comes into a man's life and has him thinking that she really loves and cares for him but doesn't because she's there for her own selfish reasons. Once she gets what she wants, she leaves him damaged while he has to pick up the pieces and pray for another woman with enough patience to help him put himself back together again. Stop acting brand new. You've been doing it to me for years and I'm dumb enough to keep letting you because unlike you I know what I want."

I wanted to call him everything but a child of God but couldn't. I wasn't proud of the way that I had treated him or the other men from my previous situationships, but what Cam didn't know was that I was actually trying. Either way love just wasn't for me because I'm a realist caught in a world of dreamers. Hell at least I wasn't trying to be the Debbie downer of love and talk people out of their beliefs. I could be one of those misguided socialist to start a cult but instead I'm trying to do my part to help.

"Go to hell Camden."

"Only if I'm following you."

I lifted my glass and threw its contents in his face. He just looked at me as if he wasn't surprised. Slowly getting up from the table he mumbled…

"I love you Trinity, take care of yourself."

I should've been chasing after him but my pride said it was just another measly argument that would stop us from talking for a few months and we would pick up where we left off as if nothing ever happened. I managed to call his name.

"Camden."

He didn't even turn around. Just continued to sweep the liquid from his shirt lifting whatever parts that weren't damp to wipe his face. I got up from the table to follow him out but couldn't seem to catch up to him.

"Cam."

He turned and I saw his hurt. My stomach dropped. I thought I would never see him in this light again, but I managed to do it. He got into his car and drove past me as if I were a figure of his imagination. I walked solemnly to my car and sat for a while with

my mind distant but my heart very present.
I heard my dad's voice whisper,

"Don't cry over spilled milk, the gallon
may still have a little left in it."
I lifted my chin and looked at myself in the
rearview mirror.

"Time to move forward because looking
back isn't where the future is."

****

"So, what you gone do?"
I literally felt like I had hit rock bottom. Here
I was scrolling a dating app looking for a
woman to just chill with. I came across one
profile that was vague but profound. "LET
ME FIX YOU."
She was beautiful and clearly got straight to
the point. Seemed to know what she
wanted.

"My dude just send her a message."
I put my hand up to silence my overly eager
homie.

"Relax. It's not that serious. I'm not
looking for a soulmate and this whole 'Let
me fix you' is a little...I don't know."

"Man, you tripping. That's what this site is
about. It's not about finding your soul mate
fool, it's just a quick set up for the time

being. Now if she happens to be the one than cool but if not then…cool."

He had a point. I was just trying to convince myself that I wasn't soul searching. I could have in-boxed a number of the females, but she was the only one that made me want to even say something.

"Alright."

My message to her was just as vague as her profile description, *'If you're up for the challenge.'*

"If you up for the challenge? What kind of line is that? Dog she gone ignore you."

"Well I guess we'll see."

"Man, whatever come on we about to miss the game."

I closed my laptop and beat him to the door.

"What you doing I'm driving?"

"Man damn I get into 3 car accidents and y'all swear I'm the worse driver alive."

"Yep! Now give me my keys."

His phone rang which was the perfect opportunity for me to grab my keys.

"Hey bae…oh for real?"

He looked over at me and I immediately knew they were up to no good. I shook my head with disapproval.

"Oh, he said he down."

"NO, I didn't! Thank you but no thank you. I'm good."

"Ok bae we on our way."

He hung up and looked at me with a mischievous grin on his face.

"Oh, hell nah. I'm staying here. You go meet your wife and her friend and y'all live it up. I'll hit the corner store and pick me up a few snacks and watch the game by my lonesome."

"Oh, come on man. Do this for me please…you don't even have to entertain ole girl. Hell, you know they not gone be paying attention to the game anyway so it's really just me and you…don't be like that."

"Man, I'm really sick of y'all playing matchmaker. What's wrong with this one? She got 6 fingers and 3 toes?"

He laughed hysterically but I was somewhat serious.

"Man come on!"

"I'm only going because I don't want to miss the game but I'm telling you if she whack…"

"Her feelings just gone be hurt… I know I know and hell I could careless because I don't know her anyway."

"Ok just as long as you know."

151

When we got to the bar his wife and her friend were already there. I was hoping we would beat them, so I would have an excuse to bounce out early, but that option was out the picture. She was beautiful true but seemed to be very timid. She glanced in our direction once and immediately turned her head as she started blushing. Her fascination was cute but old. Several times she placed her hand in the cuff of my arm rubbing my bicep. Naturally I let her, but I wasn't feeling her vibe. She complimented me a few times during the game and I returned the kind words. I noticed that when we walked in, she didn't have a drink, just a bottle of water. Didn't know what to make of it so I didn't prejudge the situation too much just figured she wasn't a drinker. When I offered the first time, she declined but I guess peer pressure got the best of her because by half time, baby girl had chugged down 3 drinks and was ordering a round of shots.

"Hey, you might want to slow down."

"Oh, I'm good. I have a pretty high tolerance level."

Strike one. To me, high alcohol tolerance is just a cute way of saying I'm an alcoholic.

"Oh…Ok."

I hit her with the sarcasm and my boy heard it.

"Aye man these boys gotta do better, I got too much riding on them tonight."

I was thankful for the change in conversation but that only brought baby girl closer to striking out. Despite the fact she was wearing a Rockets t-shirt, she knew absolutely nothing about the team.

"I think they should have left Draymond Green where he was at."

We all turned and looked at her as she casually picked up her water bottle and took a sip before realizing it wasn't her drink. I looked at my boy,

"Strike 2…."

"Awww come on dog."

I shook my head.

She reached for me again and BOOM strike 3. She threw up all over my arm and leg. I was completely disgusted. My man's wife was just as embarrassed if not pissed because she snatched her off the barstool like she was a child about to get her ass handed to her. Even though I was dripping in vomit, I tried to brace her a little from falling since she was damn near being man handled.

"Don I am so sorry. Girl stand up! Don, I promise I'll make this up to you."
She turned to the bar staff and started going off on them.

"What the hell y'all just standing there looking for? Get the man a wet towel and call somebody to clean this up! The hell…"
She made her way to the bathroom with her clearly drunk friend while Frank helped to wipe my arm off. I snatched the napkin from him.

"Dog …"
I could tell he wanted to laugh so bad.

"If you laugh, I'm going to punch you in the throat."
I got up from the stool and proceeded to the door.

"Aye man you can't leave me my car is at your place."

"Better come on or have your wife and her drunk ass friend bring you to come get it…"
He was right behind me. Once we got in the car, I took my shirt off and threw it out the window.

"Look if you, your girl or any of the homies get any bright ideas to try to hook me up…DON'T!"

He nodded. I guess this time he could sense the real in my tone. I started the car and turned my music up. I didn't want to hear anything but my boy Future.

****

'If you're up for the challenge.'

As dry as his message was, I wasn't sure if this was some kind of game or if he was really reaching out for my help and wasn't sure how to ask. Every man was a challenge for the simple fact that they all needed something different so that meant I had to wear a different hat; become a different me. I went through his profile, which again was just as dry. All of pictures he posted on his page included other guys but not one was just of him. That was an immediate flag. Not that any of them were unattractive, but who the hell was I supposed to be helping. I sat back against the couch and took a sip of wine. This time analyzing each picture. Why I was even taking the time to, I don't know but I was drawn into this message when I checked my inbox. There was one picture that I couldn't stop looking at and one man that literally popped out. I flicked through the other pictures to make sure he was in each one and he was. Whoever the mystery man was, he did a good job of making sure that his identity was well kept. Possibly to avoid embarrassment but hell I had my picture posted and I'm sure a few people I didn't want in my business were well aware that I was on here, but that would be a lie I would have to tell. I looked into the eyes of the man that captured my attention and in each one there was less excitement than his colleagues. There were pictures from what I assumed were weddings, each one where he must have been a groomsmen, but never the groom. Sporting events, parties, casual get togethers etc. but nothing that showed he had a life outside of the 3 men that surrounded him in each photo. I opted to entertain this mystery man in hopes that he wasn't close to anyone I knew even though I had never seen him around. I mean I am from a big city but small circles don't really exist in Houston. When your face is out there, someone is bound to know who you are. I replied to his message vaguely but straight to the point.

"I'm not about games. You either want me or don't…"

Reading my response over and over sounded a little raunchy so just to make sure he didn't get the wrong idea I started over.

"I'm not about games only about healing, you either need me or you don't…"
Giving my reply one last glance over I hit send. Before I could put my phone down, he had responded, this time telling me all I needed to know. Unlike Fabian I left my price out but dug deeper into his mind. I knew I was playing with fire this round but I've yet to be burned and feared nothing, "Mr.Companionship"

****

'I'm not about games only about healing, you either need me or you don't…'
It was all a big game. Optimism was non-existent and I just needed someone to get me over this hump minus my friends. She claimed to be a therapist which to me spelled out 'paid manipulator' but hell after all the hit and misses with my homeboy's trying to find me somebody why not see what she had in store for me. I laid it all out for her. I don't know if it was the alcohol or what but since she wanted to play therapist,

I was going to take my laundry to her to see if she really wanted to 'fix it'.

   I was in love. She was supposed to be my everything, but all the while belonged to a man who she barely saw. That made it easy for her to manipulate me. She was my best friend. She cooked, cleaned, maintained her own spot and never invaded my space unless I wanted her to; which she knew I always wanted her to. She asked questions no woman asked. Talked to me like she knew me and handled me when I needed to be handled. She was the female version of me. Thin filtered with her thoughts and emotionally expressive when necessary. Then she went away on a 'trip'. Started becoming distant. We made love. Not like how we normally did but something spectacular. Then she disappeared. She was my right hand. We went and did everything together. I was ready to propose until she showed up at my house with a ring that swallowed the one I had and a pregnancy test. I was confused. She broke down about needing someone and how she wasn't supposed to fall for me and some other bull that fell on deaf ears. I let her leave. Didn't chase her or even want to see her again. It's been 6 years. 6 long ass years. Damn shame how a man can let his life go by trying to fill random voids with different woman but still couldn't manage to find one that had it all. All I wanted now was a companion. Someone to have fun with that understood me but not to love. That wasn't real. If this so call therapist could fix this then, I would just be another one of her tricks.

"So…"

She didn't respond right away. And instead of giving me some bs sympathy plea of how she understood how I felt, she replied with an address to a park I was too familiar with. I gave her a thumbs up, got dressed and hoped in the car.

****

His story was all too familiar and definitely something I could handle. He was lonely. Much like my father… only he had no child. Rather than discuss the details via inbox, I wanted to look him in his face to see the seriousness in his eyes. I had been sitting on the hill reading and the park was a nice place to just think and talk and really feel the atmosphere, so I extended the invitation and he accepted. I loved the fact

159

that he knew what he wanted but disliked that he was so open to just paying for it. He made my hands-on therapy feel more like a call girl experience; this would have to change. Caught in my thoughts and pre-prep for the conversation at hand, I hadn't noticed the shadow that was now towering over me.

"Beautiful."

I smiled gingerly. Though he looked like his pictures, his approach caught me off guard.

"Donovan. Nice to meet you."

I used his hand as crutch to stand before shaking it.

"Trinity. The pleasure is mine. Have a seat."

I immediately retracted my last thought.

"I'm sorry I'm in therapist mode. What I meant was…would you like to join me?"

I gestured toward the blanket where I had been sitting. He laughed to himself,

"I'd love to."

We sat down simultaneously. For the moment, it seemed as though everything about us was in sync. So much so it scared me.

"You good?"

We never took our eyes off each other. He was very attentive.

"So just to clarify, you are 100 percent single. No children, on again off again girlfriends, hidden fiancé or wife that I should be concerned about."

"Nope."

"6 years?"

"6 years."

"No dating in between?"

"Sex. No dating. An occasion lunch here and there but only for the company. My boys tried to hook me up on several occasions, but I wasn't open to it or the women they had in mind. Look I'm here for companionship. Not looking for a girlfriend or a wife. Just someone that I can hang out with and bring to functions with my friends as a friend. I understand that this comes at a cost to me but hell at least it keeps my boys out my business and keeps me from being lonely or feeling like the odd ball."

"So, will you ever be open to love or finding someone to spend the rest of your life with?"

"Maybe but that time isn't now so, you down for the challenge Ms. Fix-it?"

He spoke freely and sarcastically.

"Absolutely but just so you know I'm not here solely as your "go to girl" when you need a date. I'm actually here to help you get to the point where you want to find someone. To tell you the truth about yourself and get back to the person who loved to love 6 years ago."

He laughed this time insultingly.

"I'm sorry did I say something funny?"

He took a breath long enough to respond.

"I'm tripping because you're really in Dr. mode."

"Well I am a doctor."

"Really?"

"Yes really!"

His questioning my truth got to me. I grabbed my bag and pulled out my wallet sized degree. Passing it to him, he examined it carefully front to back. It took everything in me not to snatch it from him and slap him with the other hand. After he was done, he apologized.

"I'm sorry. I have to admit that I thought this was some kind of game, I didn't know you were a real doctor."

"I told you it wasn't."

"True, but you don't have too many therapist shopping for clients on online dating sites. People can be whoever they want on those apps."

He had a point.

"I can understand that. Well?"

"Well what?"

"Do you still think you're being catfished?" He laughed.

"No. And again, I'm sorry for doubting but we can never be too careful now a days."

"Oh, tell me about it because you could have been a serial killer but hey, I still took a chance."

His eyes remained fixed on me. Like a school girl, I looked away and felt myself blushing. Our conversation went fairly smooth and he agreed that even though his heart wasn't set on finding someone at the moment, he would be open to it in the future.

****

So, I did it. Set myself up on a date with a therapist. I knew my boy was going to want all the scoop on everything, but I didn't want the rest of the crew in on what was really going on, so I made him promise not to say anything. Seeing as he was the most trust worthy one of us all I knew my secret was safe.

"So how much is this pussy you paying for?"

"Dog it's not like that. Ultimately, it's just a hands-on therapy session. We go on dates and hang out so she can get a feel for who I am until I find somebody else or decide that I don't need anyone."

Spitting out his beer he laughed hysterically.

"Oh, come on my dude?"

"My bad man my bad but you actually fell for the therapist gig! Dude she got you sounding like Dr. Phil."

"But check it, she's a real-life Psychologist. She showed me her mini degree and everything, I even Googled her bruh."

"So why is she on dating apps?"

"Because she doesn't advertise this portion of her business on her site. She just started this in depth, hands-on approach for brothers like me but she still takes clients at her actual office."

"Did you bother to ask why she decided to go this route? I'm saying... baby girl sound like a call girl. Is her business struggling or something because I know quite a few crazy people that need somebody to talk to."

He laughed again.

"Man look, seriously, I think she could help your boy get out this slump. She cool people. Fine as hell and I don't have to worry about what y'all gone drag into the room trying to hook me up."

"Well aye if you like it I love it. We can keep this between me and you, but you know if this don't work out, I'm going to black mail you to the grave."

We both laughed hysterically.

"Man, I'm not worried about all that. I'm just ready to play plumber ya feel me?"

"Whoa?! She gone let you do all that?"

"Only thing she said is I have to be open to the thought of a relationship. Hell, I'm trying to make the most of the experience since I'm paying for it."

"I can't believe what I'm hearing. My boy, my ace is paying for a woman."

"Negative! I'm paying for a therapist that provides hands on treatment. She's going to 'fix' me."

Even though I sounded like a jack ass, I felt like a love sick puppy.

"Man, just be careful because I would hate for this to turn into some *Thin Line Between Love and Hate* type stuff."

"It won't."

I had to take a step back and think about whether I was playing with fire. I told her that I was ready to be fixed but truth be told, I was really just looking for a fix. Just a little something or should I say someone to get me through the hard nights. Either way, she said she doesn't believe in love and neither do I at this point so I figure, no harm no foul.

"So, when you bringing your therapist to hang out with us?"

"Ha Ha. Keep it up. I don't know just yet."

"Man she's a random so no need to try to hide her from the group like she's somebody special and you don't want us to taint her image of you."

He had somewhat of a point, but they were my brothers. My family and I'm not the type to just bring anybody around my fam.

"Well when you put it that way, I don't know. What we got coming up?"

"Shoot game night. You missed the last one which was live! Have Dr. Fix it check her itinerary and make it happen cap."
I threw a paper ball at him.

"Shut up fool! I'll text her and see what's up."

****

Donovan and I hadn't gotten through our first session before he invited me to hang out with his crew and their significant others. I wanted to at least get to know him a little before I hopped right into girlfriend mode but, I did tell him that I was down for whatever he thought was necessary. When I offered to bring something, his reply was to just bring myself and he would handle the rest. I started to feel as though I was losing control of the situation between he and I but opted to address it at a later session. He picked me up from my office promptly at 8 and we headed over to his frat brothers house.

"So, are you going to brief me on each of your friends so I know what to expect? How are you going to introduce me and what should I say in response."

"Just relax this isn't a movie or stage play. Everything doesn't have to be rehearsed. Remember you're supposed to be just observing me in my atmosphere, so you can get a feel of who I am. We're just friends getting to know each other."

He was right. I shook my head in agreeance inhaled deeply and exhaled. Tonight, would be something different. Candid. Just me having a good time with someone I was getting to know. The night was that and more. I can't remember the last time I just really enjoyed myself and fit in with new people as if we had known each other our whole lives. I guess you can say I got so caught up in the night that it caught me off guard when Donovan dropped me off without even hinting or hounding about following me home for a night cap.

"So, did you enjoy yourself?"

"I did."

"You don't get out much do you?"

Sadly, I shook my head.

"I don't have very many friends so no. I just read, lounge and work."

"Well you have a new set of friends for a couple months I guess. Everybody seemed to really like you. I'm happy they didn't go in on you with the questions but I'm sure I'll have a shit load to answer later."

"Well I mean just let me know how to respond and I'm with you."

"Cool. Thanks for being my pretend date for the night and I guess I'll see you next week for our session."

"Ok, see you then."

I got out of his car and climbed into my own. Once in the silence of my own vehicle I prayed:

Father you have brought
me too far to fall now.

Grant me the strength to
focus and serve my
purpose
Without losing myself in the
process.

Tomorrow would be another day. A fresh start to get out of my feelings and into his head.

****

I had never been in a therapist office before, but it was nothing like I expected. Personally, I was digging the late night phone calls and occasional outings but I could sense that Trinity was feeling a little more personal than my liking so I suggested we get to business.

"So, what would you like to talk about?"

"You."

"Me?"

"Yeah you. I mean I've brought you into my world, so you pretty much know everything about me. Meanwhile all I know is you're a therapist that has made my life a little easier these past few weeks."

"Really. Well that's good to know. You care to elaborate?"

Right as I was about to explain how her presence has been nothing but a God send, I saw what she was trying to do.

"Oh no you don't. This isn't about me its about you."

"No this is about you. You're paying me to fix you remember? Not the other way around. My personal life is none of your concern however yours is to me so..." She was right and maybe I was the one flipping the professional switch to personal. I threw my hands up and surrendered to her statement, but being who I am I wasn't giving up on knowing her.

"Ok, you have a point. Well where do I start?"

"Wherever you like."

"I don't believe in love."

"Neither do I. What made you lose your belief in the emotion?"

"To be honest there isn't one thing in particular that I can say drove me to believe that it doesn't exist."

"Well there has to be something. Especially seeing as you were about to commit your life to someone. I'm sure you weren't going to devote your life to her because the sex was good."

"Who knows maybe..."

She laughed.

"No! I'm not buying it. There must have been something in your past that triggered it. For instance my ideal of love went out the window when I watched my mother leave me and my father."

And just like that I had her. I overheard her tell one of my friends significant other that she didn't believe in love and was trying to get back to the point where she could find something that may resemble it. I knew that if I pretended to feel the same way, she would open up like a book.

"Oh wow. Why did she leave?"

"I don't know exactly. All I know is one minute we were a full family and the next she was in tears telling me she loved me and my father and that I was all he had left. My assumption is that she was unhappy but she never expressed it to either of us."

"You think she had another man?"

"Oh no! My father was with my mom damn near around the clock. When I was at school, my mom would be with my dad at his office. They came to pick me up together, cooked and cleaned together and of course had their intimate time without me being present, so they were definitely in love."

"What makes you think it was love and not distrust?"

She was quiet for a minute.

"For two people to be around each other as much as my parents were and not argue, they had to be stupid in love."

"So, your parents never argued?"

"Of course they did, but it didn't stop them from being side by side."

I downed my head and shook it from side to side.

"What you shaking your head for?"

"Your mother left because she was being suffocated. Your father may have loved her true, but he distrusted her more."

"Excuse me?"

"Now sweetheart by no means am I trying to be disrespectful but coming from a man I'm telling you your father didn't spend all that time with your mother because he loved her, he did it to make sure that no one else could get near her."

Deep down I felt like she knew what I was saying was true, but no one had ever said it out loud for her to process. For years she lived in the denial of her parent's separation. It almost made it hard for me to move forward with her knowing how broken she was, but like she said this process wasn't about her. I was about me. My healing and health. She was a therapist, so she knew how to deal with it. Since it was my fault that the whole mood had shifted, I decided to change the dynamic of things. Not sure how she was going to take my gesture, but it was worth the try. I pulled up my music app and pressed play. *Little Brother Breaking my Heart.* An old classic hip hop song that really spoke the truth about it all. Her facial expression changed instantly as she rapped along with them.

"What you know about that?"
She sighed before responding,

"It's my favorite song. I want to say that this song and *Lil Wayne's How to Love* are the two songs that really explain a little of how I feel about the whole "love" thing.
She made air quotes with her fingers.

"So, you think all men are dogs?"

"No, but y'all most definitely have some selfish ways."

"Whoa. Be careful with that word y'all."
She laughed.

"So, Dr. Smith. What remedy do you have for me and my lack of being able to function without the company of a woman?"

"Well since you started playing therapist on me why don't you tell me what you think your problem is. I mean day one you let the bones fall out the closet, so I've been just working off that."

"What have you gathered?"

"That you're full of shit."

"Dang! Like that?"

"Please don't take any offense to how I'm saying things because you've allowed me to get comfortable with you. Just pay attention to what I'm saying. Let's start with the fact that you do believe in love. You only said that you didn't because you wanted to pick my brain."

This time I was quiet. I thought I had one upped her but apparently, she was on to me. She laughed at my silent expression. I had to laugh at myself.

"If you would have just offered the information..."

"Then you wouldn't have had to try to play me like I'm dumb? Like I don't know the ins and outs of reverse psychology? Yeah I'm damn good at what I do so better luck next go."

We laughed.

"Whatever."

"Yeah whatever. So back to what I know and what I think needs to be done."

Her sarcasm was sexy.

174

The Love Surrogate

"I know you believe in love. I know you want love, but you don't want to go looking for it, you just want it to appear on your front step like how it did for your boys. I know all of you were playboys at some point and time and just out the blue started falling in love. You thought you found your time, but you gave everything you had to the wrong woman. Now there's nothing wrong with being hurt by it but 6 years? Something tells me you're not being completely honest and open about why you haven't completely moved on. And I know for a fact that it has nothing to do with not being able to find someone because you are one of few black educated men that has it all. I know there were plenty of women your boys and their ladies have tested with you that may have been a good fit, but you saw something in each of them that wasn't right for whatever reason. I can't quite put my finger on it. Honestly, I'm clueless as to what it is exactly you're looking for because companionship comes way too easy for you."

She was right. I didn't see a mother in any of the women that I was introduced to. Every time I was introduced to a new female, I couldn't determine how good of a mother she would be to the child I wanted. They were either fun, ambitious, freaky, spontaneous whatever but they all lacked that nurturing spirit I needed. I guess my silence lasted a little too long because she interrupted my thought.

"So, you want to tell me what that is?"

"What what is?"

"The one thing that has stopped you from being in love with another woman for 6 years?"

I fought with this question for years. Unable to figure it out up until recently. I hadn't seen my ex in years but word around town was that she had been seen in the Galleria with a little girl that looks exactly like me. As bad as I wanted a child, I wanted a family more. Not the whole baby momma, baby daddy tragedy, but the husband, wife, child type of life. I looked her in the eyes. I wanted to say something but couldn't. I wasn't here for her to try to fix a broken situation with me and my ex, I was here to find a way to find a woman that I liked. That I could be satisfied with until I decided that love is something that I wanted to find me again.

"Uhhh hello? Are you going to just stare at me or answer my question?"

"My bad. If I knew I would tell you. Guess after being with the same person for 6 years, I've become very careful and selective with my taste."
She gave me the twisted lip like she wasn't buying anything I was saying.

"Seriously."

"So you're looking for another woman that's exactly like her pretty much..."

"Nah not exactly like her but fairly close." I laughed at my own honesty. I really did want another "her". I wanted my homie lover friend back. Just without the lies and complications.

"Well how will you know if you found anything similar if you don't give them a chance?"

"I do give them a chance I promise I do but..."

"But what?"

"They don't make the cut. Look is there anything wrong with me just wanting to find someone that I can do everything with without the title and emotions being attached? I mean hell isn't that what you've been doing your whole life damn near?"
I struck a nerve. She readjusted herself in her chair and tucked both her top and bottom lips in.

177

"Uh ohh the premature bad beer face."
She looked at me puzzled.

"You know the commercial with the old guy whose mouth is all sucked in after he tastes bad beer?"
Her expression didn't change.

"Oh, my goodness woman!"

"I know what you're talking about I'm messing with you."
She laughed.

"And you're right and slightly wrong all at the same time."

"How?"

"I haven't been doing this my whole life. And the men I chose to be with are given a title. They just don't get the full emotion. When they claim to love me is when everything falls apart because I can't reciprocate something I deem to be a figure of the imagination. You can feel strongly about someone but what constitutes it as being love? Love has no definition."

"Well give it one! That's the beautiful thing about it. It doesn't have a single definition. It can be whatever you want it to be. You love your job, don't you?"

"I'm passionate about helping people."
I shook my head at how difficult but sexy this woman was.

"Same thing woman!"

"Whatever back to you and what you're looking for but apparently haven't been able to find in 6 years?"

Just to end the conversation, I went into player mode.

"You."

"Boy bye!"

"No really. You're fun loving, professional, intelligent, you're a unicorn. You have and damn near know a little bit of everything without effort. You don't try to be sexy you just are. You don't try to get along you just do. Everything just comes so natural to you. All the other women just tried to damn hard to be something satisfying to me rather than just being themselves and letting me rise to the occasion."

She started to blush. Even though I didn't want her to fall too much for me, it was a bad habit for me to say all the right things to get into the right places.

"How long was your last situationship?"

"I don't know a few months."

I got up from my chair and sat in front of her. She looked me in the eyes,

"Let's go get something to eat. I could use a bite and a break. We can pick up this conversation another time."

"Cool."

I stood up and helped her from the chair. Looking into her eyes I couldn't resist myself. I kissed her full lips. She obliged.

****

"Ooo wee! I sure like the smell coming from these pots."

"Love.."

"No, I said like don't even."

She stood behind me laying her head on my back before kissing me softly. Before I had the time to turn around and kiss her back, she skipped over to the sofa and plopped down to watch me finish cooking.

"I swear you a big ass kid."

"Yep and you enjoy every minute of it."

Trinity and I have been going steady for a good 5 months now. At first, I was hesitant about accepting her advancement as my girl, but we were having such a good time that I didn't want to decline and take the chance of being lonely again. She had it all. Including the nurturing characteristic that I longed for. I knew that I was going to have

to tell her about the daughter that may or may not have been mine but never found the time to. Really no time felt like the right time. She and I were hitting it off really good and I knew that if I said something, things would go spiraling out of control and sure enough
the doorbell rang.

"I'll get it."

She jumped off the sofa and before I could stop her my heart dropped. Lindsey was standing at the door with the most precious little girl I had ever seen. She had my eyes, the smoothest chocolate brown skin with a suitcase in her hand. Trinity turned around to face me. The shock and hurt in her eyes was timeless. I wanted to hold her, but my mind was on getting to the bottom of what was really going on.

"Lindsay?! What are you doing here and how did you find me?"

"I know you know that I've been in town for a while. I was hoping that you would at least try to find me before I had to do this."

"Do what? And who is..."

"Donovan don't! She's your daughter not his."

That much could have gone unsaid, but I wasn't sure what to make of the whole

181

situation. Not only that but in the midst of our brief conversation, Trinity had been in the room gathering her things to leave.

"Trinity?! Just give me a minute."

"Clearly you have somethings to work out here so I'm going to leave."

"No! Please don't just give me a minute." I took her overnight bag out of her hand and directed her to go back into the room. Once she was out of sight, I took a few deep breaths and returned to the door.

"Come in."

I directed them to the living room and the entire time my eyes were fixed on the little girls rolling suitcase. I knew what was about to happen but couldn't stomach the thought of being a single father.

"Look Donovan I don't have much time my flight will be leaving in the morning, so I wanted to make this quick."

"Make what quick."

"She needs you Donovan and she can't live with us anymore."

"Wait. What do you mean she can't live with you anymore?"

Trinity emerged from the bedroom and grabbed the little girl's hand.

"Hey, you want to watch cartoons? Come on..."

I looked at Trinity. She never took her eyes off the little girl. They disappeared into the bedroom sliding the door closed behind them.

"It's killing my husband seeing the mistake I made."

"Mistake you made?!"

I fought back the tears and pushed through the hurt.

"You're about to leave your child because of how a man feels about what you did? Sounds to me like he's the one you should be leaving not that innocent little girl in there!"

"She'll be fine with you."

"Are you serious right now?"

I swear time was repeating itself. She stood in front of me silent, before lowering her head and walking away. I didn't try to stop her. I just let her leave.

****

This couldn't be happening. It was a nightmare that I was praying I could wake up from. After the most amazing time with the man that I finally decided to set my quest out to love, came the very moment that made me despise the word and all people thought it was really about. I felt as though I was moving in slow motion as I turned to face him. My mouth spoke the words of an empty mind. She stood there in her innocence; in the image of her father. The man that said he had no children. The liar that made me feel like love may be worth it all.

"Lindsay?! What are you doing here and how did you find me?"

I took a few steps back away from the door toward the living room. My anxiety began to kick in. As fast as I could I excused myself into the other room without being noticed. I needed to leave. As quickly as my hands would move, I gathered my things throwing them into my overnight bag. Fighting past the tears and the anger, I took one last glimpse around the room to make sure that I wasn't leaving anything behind. Once I claimed all of my belongings from his space, I made my way to the front door.

"Trinity?! Just give me a minute."

Trying to maintain my composure I responded,

"Clearly you have somethings to work out here so I'm going to leave."

"No! Please don't just give me a minute."

He took my overnight bag out of my hand and directed me back into the room. I stood there hesitantly before going back into the room as he closed the door slightly behind him. Once he went back to where they were standing I stood at the door and watched them through the crevice of the opening. My heart sank as I looked at the little girl caught in the middle of a storm. The more I watched the more my heart cried and hands trembled.

"She needs you Donovan and she can't live with us anymore."

It took everything in me not to bust through the doors and slap the dog shit out of her. My ears burned from the conversation and I refused to allow the little girl to suffer any longer. I emerged from the room and took her hand into mine.

"Hey, you want to watch cartoons? Come on..."

I saw the light in her eyes. The one that left mines years ago when my mother left me with my father without looking back. Looking me in the eyes she accepted my hand and went into the bedroom with me. Closing the door behind us I wanted to scream. I felt a tear leave my eye and wiped it away as fast as it escaped. To my surprise she had already located the remote and turned the t.v. on.

"So, what do you want to watch?"

"Barbie's dream house. It's my favorite. Does Mr. Donovan have Netflix?"

"He sure does."

We flipped through his Netflix account until she found what she wanted to watch. Meanwhile I couldn't take my eyes off her. I wondered if she knew what was going on.

"So where do you and your mother live?"

"In Vancouver with… daddy…"

She drug out the word as if she was hesitant to use it.

"I mean Steven."

She was very articulate and smart for her age.

"When are you and your mother going back."

Even though I already knew the answer to my question, I wanted to see just how clear she was about what was happening. She looked at me with tears in her eyes. I placed my hand on her leg and she immediately focused her attention back on the Tv.

"Mommy says I'm not going back. I'm staying here but she will come and see me from time to time."

My blood started to boil. Not only did this wench have the nerve to just show up on his door step, she openly explained to her daughter how she was abandoning her and leaving her with a stranger. I overheard her telling Donovan that she knew he was aware of her being in town via word of mouth and since he didn't scout her out, her dropping "their" child off like this was his fault. Either way neither of them were of my concern at this point. I immediately went into therapist mode.

"So how do you feel about not being able to go home with your mommy?"

"Sad but she said that its time that I be with my real daddy and get to love him like I love Steven."

My heart broke.

"Do you want to live here with Mr. Donovan?"

She hesitated but shook her head no.

"Are you scared?"

She shook her head yes as she wiped away the tears that were now streaming down her face.

"Can I hug you?"

She shook her head yes and reached for me. I pulled her as close as I could and embraced her the way I wished one of my father's many girl toys would have embraced me. Before long, I was sobbing with her. I tried to reassure her that I would be here whenever she needed me but hated that I didn't know the truth in my own words. This is why I vowed to never take on a client with children. I hated that he wasn't honest with me up front. How was I supposed to just walk away from this little girl? I was her and I couldn't let her be like me. She deserved a chance far more than he or I. I heard the front door close. Shortly after in walked Donovan. I couldn't disguise my anger but the look in his eyes forced me to change my demeanor.

"I'm sorry, I…"

I raised my hand, stopping him mid-sentence. I didn't want to hear it. Now was not the time for the guilt trip or give the 'see what had happened was' explanation. Turning my attention back to his now silently confirmed daughter,

"Are you hungry?"

She shook her head no.

"Are you sure? Donovan is a pretty good cook. You're more than welcome to join us for dinner."

Looking up at him with slight disgust he downed his head and spoke to her for what I assumed was the first time.

"Yeah. And if you're not hungry you can come and watch Tv in the living room, so you won't be alone back here."

She looked up at him then over at me and replied with a faint,

"Ok."

As I stood up, she walked over to me and grabbed my hand, waiting for me to lead the way. With a sad smile, I clutched her hand a little tighter and lead her into the living room. She said that she wasn't hungry because her mother fed her before they arrived at Donovan's, so rather than sitting at the table, he and I joined her in the living room and watched movies until she dozed off. He scooped her precious frame out of the chair and laid her in the guest room. Watching him with her warmed my heart but chilled my spine at the same time. I knew there was no waiting to talk later so when he returned from tucking her in, I prepared myself and took a few deep breaths.

"Look Trinity, I didn't know she was mine."

"I asked if there were any possibilities as well and you clearly lied."

"I didn't lie."

"So, what do you call it? Withholding truth?"

"I don't expect you to understand."

"I'm a therapist. Try me."

He sat silently for a minute before speaking,

"It wasn't supposed to be like this.."

"I understand how my position in your life now has complicated things, but in the beginning I made it clear that this was not a game. That I wasn't here to play with your emotions or create a feeling that didn't already exist but you…"

With an attempt to lower my now accelerated voice, I took a deep breath in the middle of my thought.

"Now it all makes perfect sense."

"What makes sense?"

"You never really had plans on fixing you. You only hired me to hang out with. You knew that if I knew you had a daughter than I wouldn't continue to 'counsel' you and you didn't want to be alone all over again."

There was truth in my words, and he confirmed with his silence yet again. I stood up and headed to his bedroom to get my things. He followed behind me.

"The last time I saw her she had a ring on her finger and what may have been a pudge in her stomach. She was married the entire time we were dating. When she moved I knew nothing. She doesn't have social media, so I didn't know anything about her being born, what she looked like, NOTHING! Hell up until tonight I didn't even know her name."

"What is her name?"

"Nya."

"Nya…wow."

"Wow what?"

I turned to face him.

"Her name. Her name is Swahili for friend or companion."

He looked at me dumbfounded before putting 2 and 2 together.

"That's crazy."

"Yeah it is."

"So, what does this mean for us?"

I was speechless and wasn't sure how to respond. I wish he would have been honest in the beginning. I wish he would have let me leave when I had the chance. I wish I would have never looked her in the eyes. I wish I knew how to love. I knew that Nya would need guidance at some point, but with Donovan's friends, she had more than enough aunties to love her the way she needed.

"I don't know."

"What do you mean you don't know?"

"Just like I said, I don't know. None of this was in the plan. I was supposed to counsel you and you were supposed to be able to enjoy life alone until you were able to find someone to live it with...but then this happened. We happened, she happened so, I don't know."

"I understand. Well allow me to pay you for the remainder..."

"Are you serious right now?"

He looked at me as if he were clueless as to why I was upset.

"Did you just offer to pay me? When I'm sitting here thinking that you and I are in a relationship?"

"I'm sorry I didn't mean it like that. Look nothing I'm saying or doing is coming out right. Maybe we can just start over tomorrow."

"Yeah maybe."

I grabbed my bag and proceeded toward the door. Right as I was walking past him, he grabbed my arm and whispered into my lips.

"I'm sorry for everything. If I knew this was going to happen then I wouldn't have allowed things to change between us."
He kissed my lips without my reciprocation. Pressing his forehead into mine,
"I still need you Trinity."
I stepped away from him and left him standing in the doorway of his bedroom.

****

I fell asleep in the chair in the guest bedroom watching her sleep. I woke up to the sound of the toilet flushing. For some reason I was hoping last night was just a bad dream but when she emerged from the bathroom with her toothbrush in her hand, I realized just how real things really were.
"Good morning Mr. Donovan."
"Good morning. You hungry?"
Timidly, she shook her head yes. I went into the kitchen and realized that I didn't have many breakfast foods because Trinity and I always made smoothies before our run and would go and get breakfast afterward. I could feel her looking at me while I searched the fridge for something quick to cook.

"Can we have donuts? Mommy never got me donuts. Only at school. Sometimes."

"I take it you like donuts."

She shook her head vigorously.

"Ok donuts it is. But don't get to comfortable with eating too many ok?"

She smiled and let out a light hearted

"Ok."

"Ok. Go put on your shoes."

She ran into the guest room and came out with her rain boots on. I couldn't help but laugh to myself.

"Those are nice but it's not raining outside. As a matter of fact, your feet are going to get really hot in those. How about you put on a pair of tennis shoes or some flip flops."

She looked at me confused. It never dawned on me that because she lived up north for her entire life, she may not own a pair of sandals so had no idea what a flip flop even was. Instead I didn't pull her out of her element but agreed to just let her do her. This parenting thing was definitely going to be new to me.

"On second thought you can just wear those. We're not going to be out long anyway."

I went into the room slid my feet into my slides and headed for the door. Opening it slightly we were greeted by Trinity who was just about to knock.

"Well isn't this a pleasant surprise. Good morning gorgeous."

She immediately turned her attention off of me and replied,

"Good morning Nya."

"Good morning."

I can't lie I felt some type of way but due to the circumstance, I let it go. True enough she and I started this little relationship thing but at the same time I thought she understood ultimately it was a part of the process. As a matter of fact, I hadn't even talked to my boys about last night's fiasco but needed to get with them as soon as the smoke cleared.

"I wasn't interrupting anything was I?"

"No. Actually I was just about to take Nya for breakfast. You're more than welcome to join us."

"Really because I was thinking nothing is better than some donuts and chocolate milk."

She pulled a box of donuts out of her bag and a can of nestle chocolate. I looked down at Nya whose face was completely lit up.

"Well that saves us a trip because it's exactly what she wanted."

"Good."

This time she looked me in the eyes and kissed me. Never taking her eyes off mine. I took her bag from her hands and directed her to come in. She followed Nya into the living room who had found the remote and turned on her favorite cartoon. I grabbed the milk out the fridge along with a few glasses and placed the donuts on the warmer. Walking into the bedroom I pulled my phone out and group texted my boys.

I need my brothers ASAP! #911

They all responded almost simultaneously.

Bet!

I'm down brother just say when.

You good homie? Whats up?

Shit is crazy but let's meet tonight. The spot. Around 7

That works for me

I'm there

Cool! See yall then.

I hadn't realized Trinity was standing in the door way behind me. She finished the chocolate milk and handed me the mug.

"You ok?"

"Yeah, just need to talk to the boys." She nodded as if she already knew what I was going to say.

"She can stay here with me or maybe I can take her back to my place and she and I can talk."

"She seems to be taking her mom leaving her pretty good."

"She's definitely a smart kid but she's introverted like me. She may be hiding it or just used to not being around her mom, so her absence is common. Either way, I really don't think she understands the depth of what's happening. Hell, none of us do."

"True. Well what do you think I should?" She downed her head and nodded it slightly, hesitantly she responded,

"I'll just take her back to my place. Give her a little girls night. Do her hair and just talk to find out what she knows and how she feels."

"Ok, cool. Thanks Trinity. You don't have to do all this, but I appreciate you for stepping in and helping me and my daughter the way you are."

I could tell my calling Nya my daughter struck a nerve in her but me calling Nya my daughter out loud was me taking my first step into being the man that I was supposed to be to the little girl in the other room.

"What time are you meeting the guys?"

"7."

"Ok well after we finish the donuts and watch a little t.v, I'll leave so I can get things together and you can either drop her off or I can come and pick her up whichever you prefer."

"I'll just drop her off on my way to the spot and pick her up on my way back home."
"Or both of you can just stay the night at my house."

I didn't want to crush her spirits, but I wasn't sure if I wanted to continue with whatever this relationship was. Truth be told, it started on a lie and rather than letting my bones fall out one by one, I rather just let the light shine.

"No. I'll just come get her. I don't plan on drinking, but you know my boys are my outlet and right now is when I need them most."

She could sense what I was getting at without me even saying it.

"I'm not forcing the relationship between us, but I just think it would be healthy for her to be in the same atmosphere here like back at home with her mother and her husband. She's used to seeing a man and woman together."

I was getting a little irritated by Trinity's 'I know and have all the solutions attitude' but rather than burst her bubble I stood stern with my decision.

"As much as I appreciate your help, I think I know what's best at this moment. So, I'll come and get her after I hang with the boys for a little while. We're meeting early, so I won't be out too late. 9-9:30 at the latest."

Rather than rebuttling like she always does to get her way, she just walked away. With a fake smile, I followed behind her and sat on the couch next to my future.

****

¨My boy!! What's up where you been?¨
¨Playing house with Trinity.¨

I gave Ken the look because he was the only one that knew the real behind Trinity and me. He laughed.

"No but for real what's up. You hit us 911. Everything good?"

I shook my head.

"So, what you need to talk about?"

"Lindsay."

"Lindsey? Oh, hell nah! Dog look, you and Trinity seem to be hitting it off nice, don't tell me you've been trying to look for her again."

"No! She found me."

"You playing, right?"

I shook my head and they all looked at me as if I had left them hanging.

"She was mine."

"She?"

"The baby she was pregnant with when she left. Apparently, it was a little girl and she's mine."

"Dude wait...pause. When did you find this out?"

"Last night when she dropped her off."

"Dropped her off? Wait Lindsay was here?"

I noticed that my boy Chris was quiet and didn't seem to be as interested in the conversation as everyone else was. He felt my stare and surrendered.

"Man, I was going to tell you she was in town but when I thought about your vibe with Trinity, I didn't want to bring that drama back. But real talk when I saw her, she didn't have anyone with her, so I never saw the little girl. I thought it was just her."

"Man, so you just now telling us you knew she was here? Why didn't you tell us?"

"Because I knew y'all would tell him and like I said it feels good to see my boy happy and consistent."

Everybody immediately went in on him and I stopped them.

"C, I appreciate you for looking out but dog you shouldn't have let me be blindsided like that."

"My bad, so what happened and what you mean she dropped her off."

I gave everybody the brief story of how me and Trinity had been chilling at the crib before the shit hit the fan. The whole table was silent.

"So, what you gone do?"

"What the hell you mean what am I going to do? I don't have any choices! I'm a father so I have to be a father."

"I know that man but how did Trinity take it?"

"To be honest..."

I couldn't say what I wanted to say right off the bat, but my boy Ken knew where I was going.

"It's complicated."

"What she doesn't want to be with you anymore? I thought she was the ride or die type. She seems like she good with kids. Hell, she always out with Denna and her nieces."

"Yeah but this is different man."

"How?"

He just wouldn't let up. I finally broke down and told the truth.

"Trinity was only supposed to be my therapist."

"Therapist?"

They all looked at me like they had been bamboozled. Ken chimed in and told the story the best he could.

"Look we all know our boy needed help finding somebody and he found Trinity. Turns out Trinity is more hands on with her practice and they ended up falling for each other a little more than expected. Well, he claims she ended up falling for him but we all see and know different. Anyway, one of her number one rules when it comes to hands-on treatment is no kids and well...Donovan never told her the details about Lindsay so...here we are."

"Dog you been fooling with an escort?"

"She's not an escort!"

"I can't tell. You're paying a woman to hang out with you and I know y'all sleeping together so she's a damn escort."

I really wanted to snatch him, but it wouldn't change the conversation, so I just stared him down until he fell back.

"So, are y'all together or not? And where is the little girl now?"

"I don't know."

"You don't know where the little girl is? What the..."

"No! I don't know if me and Trinity are together like that and Nya is with her right now."

"Like that? Explain."

"This was all a game to me at first then she started falling for me and I lowkey started falling for her but I refuse to get hurt again. To be honest I don't know everything about her when it comes to her past relationships. This thing me and her got going right now is kind of real but not really. Look, it's hard to explain."

"Fool what?!"

I ignored his response because I wanted to choose my words carefully when talking about me and Trinity's situation.

"So...Nya huh?"

"Yeah."

I filled them in on more of the conversation between me and Lindsay and how Trinity has been acting since the unfortunate reunion.

"Do you want to be with her?"

"I don't know. There's a lot of things about Trinity that y'all don't know and I prefer to keep it that way but at the same time, it's making it hard for me to even feel anything for her. I mean she got me out my funk and we have so much fun together but when I brought the family thing to her attention she bugged out. She doesn't believe in love so how can I trust her with me or my child's emotions. I mean realistically I can't."

"But how do you know that if you haven't given her a chance?"

"In case you haven't noticed dude, were talking about people's lives and even though I'm willing to gamble with mine, I refuse to let another woman walk out my child's life like her own mother did."

The passion in my voice scared the hell out of me. I never knew that being a father could pull this type of reaction out of me. Even though I wanted to be with Trinity genuinely, my circumstances changed the way I looked at the bigger picture. I couldn't take a chance with her and it was time to cut ties all together. I just wasn't sure how to do it.

"I think you're making a mistake. I mean I know how things started with you and Trinity but it's clear she's trying to be there for you and baby girl so I think she deserves a chance. Plus, what do you know about raising a little girl? Lindsay was dead wrong for this and that's real talk."

"Well I can't move backwards and that's what I have my boys and their girls for right? Uncles and aunties?"

"Oh, you know we got your back big dog and of course the ladies are going to love this but at the end of the day you're the father."

"Yeah I know."

We all sat quiet for a minute. Each taking a sip. Ken lifted his glass and we all followed suit.

"To Donovan and our new niece Nya."

I was on the verge of tears, but it felt good knowing I had my brothers if I didn't have anybody else.

****

"Nya, are you almost done?"
I made sure Donovan brought her night bag so that she could bathe while at my house. Even though he said they wouldn't be staying the night, when I left his place, I went and picked up a few things from the store to make the guest room feel a little more 'child-like.'
"Yes maam."
Hearing her voice warmed me up. Despite the fact I was hurt by not knowing the truth up front, I couldn't turn back.
"Do you need me to help you?"
"No, I got it."
"You sure?"
"Yes."
I smiled to myself. I thought about how when I was her age, my mom would always treat me like a baby, as if I was incapable of bathing myself and getting ready for bed. It was crazy how much of me I saw in her. She came out of the bathroom with her dirty clothes in hand. I took them from her and

gathered the rest of the things out of the bathroom.

"If you want you can go to the table, I cut some fresh fruit for us to eat while we watch movies."

"Thank you."

"You're welcome sweet heart."

"I miss my mommy."

And just like that my heart shattered in my chest. Her words were dry. Empty almost. There was no real emotion behind them which scared me.

"I'm sorry."

I couldn't think of anything else to say besides 'I'm sorry.' Without saying another word I kneeled down in front of her and took her hands into mine.

"Everything is going to be ok. I know you miss your mom but I'm sure you'll see her again soon."

She shook her head no. At this point I wasn't sure what to say. She responded for me.

"She told me that it would be a while before she saw me again, but she loves me and always will. It's Donovan's turn to be my daddy."

I felt myself tearing up but held it in.

"She's right. It is."

"What about you?"

"What do you mean what about me?"

"Are you going to be my other mommy?" Before I had the chance to respond there was a knock at the door.

"Hold that thought…"

Grateful to see his face,

"Hey. How was boy's night?"

"It was good. Got a lot of things off my chest and you know it's always good to have your close friends around when you need them most."

"This is very true."

I could tell there was something on his mind and offered him to come in. He refused.

"I think its best if I just get Nya and we head on home."

"Well we weren't expecting you for another hour, so she just got out the tub."

Reluctantly, he came in and sat at the bar.

"Is there something on your mind you want to talk about?"

"There is but to be honest I don't know how to say it or even if I want to."

Since he refused to address the elephant in the room and I could sense what was going to be said I started the very necessary conversation.

"Nya is going to need therapy and I'm more than willing to offer my services since she's already familiar with me."

The look of aggravation covered his face.

"I appreciate you being a doctor but how about being human?"

I was puzzled by what he meant.

"She needs love. Plenty of it. Not somebody to pick her brain to see how to 'fix' her. She doesn't have a problem that needs to be solved. She's in a different environment that's going to take some time getting used to. With all due respect, I thank you for everything you've done for me. All the fun, laughs, and genuine intimacy. The chemistry we have makes it hard for me to say this but Trinity,"

He walked over to me and kissed my forehead before finishing,

"I have to raise my daughter on my own or until I meet a woman that can love us both, which I know is something you're not ready for or you're not capable of."

I felt my heart in my stomach. I had to admit to myself there was some truth in his statement, but I also knew that in the little time I spent with him, I found myself changing. Not enough to say that it was love, but then again because I never opened myself up to it, I couldn't say what I was feeling.

"Exactly."

"No wait. I am capable, I just..."

"Just what? And you think this would be a healthy environment for my child?"

"The child you lied about?"

"The child I didn't mention because I wasn't sure about."

Nya stood at the door with her bag. I hated that she had heard the conversation between me and Donovan. I could only imagine the way she was feeling. Donovan walked over to her and kneeled at her side.

"You ok?"

She shook her head. I chimed in.

"Did you want to stay or are you ready to leave?"

Donovan turned and starred at me. I looked at her and she looked at me...

"I..."

She turned and looked at Donovan.

"I..."

Her voice quivered from the tears.

"I want to go home."

Donovan scooped her up in his arms. He turned and faced me. Solemnly he spoke,

"Goodbye Trinity."

The Love Surrogate

Deep down I screamed his name, but nothing came from my lips. It was as though he was moving in slow motion as he turned around and was leaving. I was reaching for him, running to him but my feet were planted in the same place. My eyes became heavy and loosened as I heard the door close behind them. The tears made streams down my face and ended with a puddle in the crevice of my lips.

****

It was me. All me. With every client I helped, I lost a little of myself. Camden was right. I grew insecure not knowing whether there was a man out there that could make me feel more than the self-worth I had built on my own. A man with the patience to build a new me with the old materials of my past life and really make me whole again. I too was needy. Eager and willing to make a living off the pain of men that were just as imperfect as myself. Most importantly exchanging my intellectual property for the sake of a dollar and touch of his hands, lips or the stiff extension from his inner thighs. I yearned for companionship. To be someone's everything. To escape feeling alone at night without being attached emotionally but craving that physical attention that didn't start between my legs. I cared for his daughter. There was no doubt in my mind that I was willing to pour a little of me into her. The girl that needed her mother. That was open for guidance and wanted someone to teach her every virtue a woman holds. He took that from me. I lent the rest with each coming and going with each "client" I took on. Now…who could feel the voids in me? I made each of them love me and hate me at the same time. I convinced myself that this was only work. I gave birth to feelings and gave them willingly to be nurtured by women other than myself because they deserved it. Each man deserved it. I poured myself another shot. Self-injected epidural. I needed to be numb before I could consider pushing out anymore of me and walking away. I felt a hand on my shoulder and familiar voice in my ear.

"Trinity…what's up? You good?"
Attempting to fix myself up, I entertained the voice that I thought I had left behind.

"Joseph. What are you doing here?"

"I should be asking you that since you're sitting over here with a bottle and a shot glass all alone? What's this all about?"

He lifted the half empty bottle and looked at me with disappointment.

"Don't tell me..."

"...I won't."

He downed his head in pity for me.

"So, are you going to tell me what you're doing here? Kind of far from home aren't you?"

"Meeting one of my frats for drinks and to hang out...matter of fact..."

He turned towards the door and I mimicked his movement. My heart instantly started beating in my throat. Camden. Walking towards us he seemed puzzled but slightly excited to see me despite the terrible goodbye we last shared.

"Cam...."

"Trinity."

Joseph looked back and forth between us confused.

"Y'all know each other?"

Looking directly at me Camden responded,

"Remember that talk we had back in college...about the one that I couldn't let go of?"

"Yeah I remember."

213

"Well here she is."
Joseph looked back and forth between Camden and I again before resting his eyes on me.

"Oh, ok my bad."
Camden and I never took our eyes off of each other, but I could feel Joseph staring at me.

"It's all good. Been a minute since I've seen or talked to her. She's a really busy woman."

I wanted to say something back in return to his smart comment but didn't.

"Is that right?"

"Yep but..."

He playfully grabbed Josephs shoulder,

"...this one is off limits brother. You have to find yourself another beauty because this one is mine. Has been since diapers."

"Oh really?"
Joseph kept his eyes on me and spoke with a jealous tone,

"That's funny because I've had the pleasure of getting to know her already."

Camden turned and looked at Joseph for a brief second before focusing on me again.

"Oh, you know her too?"

"Yeah we met..."
I cut him short.

"I met him back in Dallas at a therapist's conference, while I was looking for a therapist."

Joseph looked at me with shame in his eyes, but I couldn't let Camden know the truth of what had transpired between me and Joseph. It was all starting to make sense. Why I was so attracted to Joseph and why he reminded me so much of Camden. They were almost one and the same. Camden stood at my right side, Joseph remained at my left.

"I would offer you a drink but looks like you beat me to the punch."

"She has both of us beat."

"Yeah, I'm just about done. It was good seeing you again Joseph...Camden."

I grabbed my blazer off the back of the chair, took one last shot and headed for door.

"Trin!"

Camden followed me to the door.

"I'm not about to let you drive after the way that bottle looked."

"I'm a big girl. I can take care of myself."

"I know you are but its time you let someone else do that. Not to mention your safety isn't the only one at stake right about now."

The last thing I wanted was a lecture from Camden about being a hypocrite and driving drunk after all the times I got on him about it, but I really wasn't in the mood to be around him after the craziness. I got a text on my phone from Joseph.

What we don't know can't kill us. Just wish I knew before I fell for you too...

I immediately closed my phone and looked at Camden.

"I'll call an uber and come get my car in the morning."

"That's not necessary T, I'm taking you home and ubering back."

Before I had the chance to rebuttle, he had my keys in his hand and was waving to Joseph that he would be back. Joseph never took his eyes off me. Looking away from him, Camden wrapped his arm around my shoulder and brought me into him. I welcomed his gesture and wrapped my arms around his waist as he opened the door and directed me out. Once we were in the car, my emotions poured out of me like the liquid courage that went in.

"Why can't I be human? Why can't I love the way people say they love me? That little girl needs me! I can't let her be like me. I can't, I can't stomach the thought of another child being abandoned and not knowing her full potential all because her mother was too much of a coward to play with the cards she was dealt."

He sat quiet and didn't interrupt. Just rubbed my back as a sobbed and screamed my frustrations through the tears.

"Why didn't she love me enough to take me with her? Why can't, why can't I live a normal life!"

"You can Trin...just..."

He stopped and held my face in his hands.

"I knew that you trying to help everybody else would lead to this breakdown and even though I tried to let you do it on your own, I couldn't. Part of this is my fault."

"What do you mean?"

"Fabian."

I was confused and shocked at the same time.

"Wait how do you know about Fabian?"

He pulled out his phone and pulled up his text messages between Mr. Insecure and his younger brother.

"You set me up?"

"It wasn't hard. I know you T. Better than you know yourself sometimes. I figured if I set this up, I could control the outcome and keep you safe. Look that's not important."

"The hell it isn't! How? I mean why did you do this?"

"Because, I needed you to see what you would be getting yourself into. I talked to Fabians brother, found out his situation, found the profile you created and we set it up. I was only able to control the situation for so long. You weren't supposed to end up in Dallas you were supposed to be back home with me."

"And Joseph?"

"What about him?"

"You sent him too?"

"No! He never came to mind when you said you were in Dallas."

I wanted to think it was a lie, but I could sense it wasn't.

"Trinity, I knew Fabian would see what I saw in you. And I also knew that I had to take a chance of losing you but that was the chance I had to take. But I knew... I... I KNOW this is meant. I told you that I couldn't watch you self-destruct and I tried to prevent it but in typical Trinity fashion you couldn't leave well enough alone. I know you was falling for him and when you called me from Dallas, I knew you was going to give it up, but you didn't. I couldn't protect you. Trinity, you have something that a lot of women wish they had and that's true love. True. Genuine. Love. Let it be your gift sweet heart and not your curse. You are not your past but the product of pressure. A diamond."

For the first time in a long time I heard him. I felt every word. With each cut, I was resurrected into something more beautiful. It was time to accept the things that I could not change. With my eyes full of tears, I stared into his eyes,

"I love you."

His words made my heart skip a beat,

"I…"

He placed his finger over my lips,

"Let's go home."